THE
SALT
GROWS
HEAVY

Cassandra Khaw

NIGHTFIRE

TOR PUBLISHING GROUP
New York

THE SALT GROWS HEAVY

A Nightfire Book
Published by Tom Doherty Associates / Tor Publishing Group
120 Broadway
New York, NY 10271

tornightfire.com

Nightfire™ is a trademark of Macmillan Publishing Group, LLC.

The Library of Congress Cataloging-in-Publication Data
is available upon request.

ISBN 978-1-250-83091-3 (hardcover)
ISBN 978-1-250-32296-8 (signed edition)
ISBN 978-1-250-90551-2 (Canadian)
ISBN 978-1-250-83092-0 (ebook)

Our books may be purchased in bulk for promotional,
educational, or business use. Please contact your local bookseller
or the Macmillan Corporate and Premium Sales Department
at 1-800-221-7945, extension 5442, or by email at
MacmillanSpecialMarkets@macmillan.com.

First Edition: 2023
First Canadian Edition: 2023

Printed in the United States of America

0 9 8 7 6 5 4 3 2 1

For Jeff Solomon,
this is what you get for not giving up on me

I

The First Night

"Where are you going?"

I pause. In the penumbra, the fading dusk gorgeted by coral and gold, you could be forgiven for mistaking the ruined house a ribcage, the roof its tent of ragged skin. The foundation, at a careless look, could pass for bones, the door for a mouth, the chimney a finger crooked at the sky, or at a wife who would not be a savior.

Ash sleets from the firmament in soft handfuls of black, gathering in gauzy drifts around my ankles. The sky is ink and seething murk, whispering secrets to itself, the clouds snarled like long, dark hair. I glance into the house. Two of my daughters look back, eyes shining. They are seated astride a twitching form, its limbs too small to have belonged to an adult. Like cats, they croon to one another even as they nibble their fins and fingertips clean. My breath snags. Only days old but already, they are the best of their parents. They have their father's full lips, his blue eyes, his supple sun-warmed skin.

And they have *my* teeth, my deepwater hair, like the lures of the anglerfish spun into thick coils. Nothing sticks to those radiant strands, no amount of gore or mud. Which is fortunate, given how messily my offspring eat.

One fishes a gnawed-down fingerbone from her maw, flicks it to the ground. The other pounces and for a moment, I glimpse the fair circle of their victim's face; its eyes gouged, its cheeks flensed, its skull emptied of sweetbreads. Mermaids—especially those born half-prince—leave nothing to waste.

"Of course. I forgot. You can't speak. My apologies."

I look back. The plague doctor flutters a hand, voice strange behind their mask. Today, they are dressed most austerely: plain black robes; a broad-brimmed hat; the half-skull of a vulture, carefully bleached, unornamented save for a single hieroglyph embossing its brow. Alone of my husband's people, what few remain after the apocalypse of my children's hunger, the plague doctor is not afraid. Has not ever been afraid. "Do you know where you're going?"

I consider the question. I'd toyed with the idea of going home. In my dreams, I still swim that soundless black, still travel its eddies of salt and cold nothing. My sisters are alive in these nocturnal fantasies: colorless, resplendent, their hair floating like a frothing of wedding veils.

But those are just baseless images pieced together by the unconscious, invoked by a longing that has since had time to turn septic. I have been on dry land for too long; the depths would devour me the way they would any creature of the air.

"Well?" The plague doctor steps closer, fearless. Eyes green as the humid, hated summer.

I shrug.

To my astonishment, they laugh.

"Such a pair we make. I don't know what I'm going to do either, what with the kingdom being eaten to nothing." The look they slide me—heavy-lidded and coquettish—is so auda-cious that I soundlessly laugh in spite of myself. "If you don't know where you're going, do you at least know what you plan to do?"

I shrug again. Over the snow-gilded mountains, I know there are kingdoms without number, pastoral and beautiful, each ruled by another prince or king, another czar and his court of calm-eyed lackeys. Another man like my husband: beautiful and terrible and cocksure in the magic he'd thieved from his bride.

There. I could go there, perhaps. Find another sovereign who'd fish a mute from the waters, who'd marry her, bed her, murder her sisters for a superstition, and then pry the teeth from her gums for the sake of caution. I could find one of those again, maybe, and wait until my daughters come to gnaw his country down to its bones.

As though conscious of my musings, the plague doctor nods, their voice hollowed by the fluted bone. Even after all this time, I cannot tell whether they are male, female, neither, both, some gradient wicking between definitions. "And you shall know her by the trail of dead."

A harpy phrase. I smile at the music of it.

"How do you feel about company?"

I cock my head.

"A doctor is always useful," they tell me, fox-sly. "What do you say?"

I say nothing, of course. My husband cut the tongue from me when he discovered I was pregnant; braised it with five-spice and saffron before feeding me the tender slivers. Animal meat was forbidden, but assisted autosarcophagy, his soothsayer had crooned, would ensure pliance.

But I smile, nonetheless, and it is answer enough for my new companion.

~

We burned the kingdom to cinders. Pillars of choking smoke rose from the bodies we'd heaped into neat stacks, stinking fattily, saltily of crisping pork. The plague doctor had insisted. To leave the bodies as they were was to invite disease, an epidemic that would rot the soil, infect the waters.

"What is the point of revenge if you can't enjoy it?" The plague doctor chuckled as they led me and my chocolate-stippled horse—my husband's last gift before our children made a feast of him: a sullen gelding who loathed him as much as I did—from the smoldering ruins.

I offered no reply and instead watched the smoke, like warnings of what would be.

~

In winter, as in the spring, the taiga is beautiful. Pine trees and white spruce scrape at the firmament, skeining the snow in strange patterns. There are smaller plants too, aspen and alder and birch, even colonies of withered ferns. Occasionally, I catch sight of wolves in the tree line, shark-sleek and grey; of bobcats glaring yellow-eyed from some desecrated barrow; of foxes, their muzzles sodden and dripping with red.

The plague doctor's breath plumes through the air as we walk. Mine does not. Though I hold no particular affection for it, the cold has never been a thing I fear, a fact that once amused my husband's court to no end. They made me promenade through the winter, my naked skin irridescing with frost. Still, my companion insists on swaddling me in fur: woolly gloves and a bearskin coat of unusual pallor.

"It would look strange if you weren't dressed for the weather," the plague doctor says in way of explanation as I fondle my gifts, the lining smelling of musk and frankincense oil. The fur itself is almost satiny, a delight to massage between my fingers. "People would ask questions."

I scan the wilderness. There is no one but the hares and the badgers here, nothing but the trees and the quiet, the hawks and the wights—the unsleeping dead, burning forever, unable to rest—pacing spindle-limbed through the gloom. If there are men concealed in the boughs, they harbor no interest in our acquaintance. For fear of my plague doctor, perhaps.

Or me.

The plague doctor laughs, arsenic-sharp, a bark of a noise, before crunching into a bright red apple. "A stranger is an easy target, easier still when they are as strange as you. If you had believed our former kingdom cruel, a place of treachery, let me assure you that it was the finest of its neighbours. The rest of them—"

Something of a smile emerges, a private amusement.

"Anyway. Yes. The furs should help. At least until you smile. Your teeth will give us away immediately," the plague doctor murmurs as they chew, their voice softer, kinder. "I'm surprised that your tongue didn't grow back with them."

I shrug. The physiology of my species is protean, unmetered by logic. When we breed with angels, our children accrete feathers. When we lay with hurricanes, we birth storms, windspirits with the voices of dead sailors. A thousand mythologies contributed to my conception. Who can say which of them was responsible for this miracle? I stroke the stump of my tongue—enough has regrown so that I might separate bitterness from salt, might savor the taste of muscle, briefly seared—over my back teeth, tracing the needle-thin growths, and shrug again, more empathically than before.

In answer, the plague doctor guffaws, a vulpine sound this time. There is no more conversation after that. We stop, once or thrice, to attend to the little shrines that dot the woods, half buried in the snow. Wax clogs their hearts like colored tendons, the corpses of a thousand candles. Food rots without, untouched by the forest.

"I don't believe in souls," the plague doctor whispers at one point, voice husked, and I suspect the words are intended for someone else, sometime else, a place and a moment as distant from the present as I am from the sea. They extract a feather—black as pitch save for its meridian of fire—from a satchel and place it atop the melted tallow. "But just in case: a feather to help them fly home."

Theirs is the only feather amidst the despoiled charcuterie, the mould-spotted breads. I do not ask why, or what, or how the plague doctor expects the spirit to ascend on a single plume of ebony. Even if I had the voice to do so, I would not have. This is not my grief to split from throat to belly, not my past to reconstruct from viscera and ice.

And besides, who am I to speak on this? All of my kind are just souls with a cloak of skin and scales, barely tethered to the act of living.

We walk until the moon reaches its zenith, a cataracted eye glowering from the star-drowned sky. Then, at a clearing, a square of land jagged with old cairns and vacated graves, its denizens either cannibalized by the forest or changed by it, my travelmate declares:

"We'll stop here."

I dismount with the plague doctor's assistance, out of courtesy rather than any actual need. Parturition has not weakened me. If anything, it has done the reverse. But these small courtesies seem to please my companion so I perform these rites as a small concession. A trade for services rendered.

In the distance, something moans, low and displeased; a wolf, maybe, or a daughter of mine, sharp-teethed and jeweled with onyx scales, already grown bored of her butchered kingdom. The stars blink out, one after another, eaten by the rising fog.

Still, whatever it might be, the plague doctor evidences no interest in its existence, divvying up our responsibilities with a noncommittal authority. I am placed in charge of the fire, of this evening's meal. The plague doctor tasks themself with everything else: defenses, the replenishment of our rations, the ablutions of my mount.

Mine are easier duties than I'd anticipated despite my inex-
perience with the world, my husband having kept me cloistered:
a bloody jewel swaddled in the dark. I have an unerring sense
of which branches serve better as kindling, and which are still
green and wet at their heart. The fire comes quickly too, a flash
of orange-gold, lunging for me like a lover thrice denied.

For food, I roast us the trout that the plague doctor supplies.
The meat is clumsily seasoned: some dried thyme, some basil
crushed under a jag of rock, a rich spill of peppercorns, before
it is then cooked with too much eagerness, too little skill, and
not enough sense.

"It's edible. I wouldn't worry too much," remarks the plague
doctor later as they pick chunks of black-burnt meat from their
share; first examining the charred meat by the darting flame-
light before tossing it into the snow. Once they have whittled
the ash away, they eat. I devour mine whole, ash and bones
and all.

When we finish eating, we lapse into silence, one watching the other. The fog deepens and the firelight smears orange
across the plague doctor's mask.

"What?" They laugh, low and rich.

I rap the bridge of my nose.

Fingers rise to the vulture beak, trace the wicked swoop of
its mandible. "The mask?"

I nod. In all the time we've known one another, I've never
seen the physician without the cover of another creature's shell.
They laugh, the sound refracted by keratin. Without a word,
the plague doctor removes their mask and their hat, dragging
fingers through a dense mass of close-cropped black curls. The

face underneath is raptorial: sharp angles, a mouth predisposed towards wryness, the eyes glittering and thick-lashed. Not unattractive, not unhandsome, but curiously barren of the phenotypes that mark the human species, androgynous in a way that makes me think of dolls and polished, hand-carved things.

When the plague doctor turns their head, I see something else: careful stitching along their jaw and cheekbones, the hollows of their orbital sockets. Stitching so fine that it could be invisible. Almost.

They grin at me, knowing. Their voice too could belong to anyone, any gender. "You have questions?"

I take the mask from their hands and rotate the polished rostrum, finger mapping its topography of ravines and muslin netting. Once, this might have held camphor and dried flowers, a fragrance of cinnamon. Glass in the eye sockets. But for some reason, the plague doctor saw fit to maim the design. I wonder what the halving of it symbolizes.

"I'll trade you." The plague doctor slithers closer, their robes dragging across the snow. I inhale their scent: a dry, faint potpourri of herbs, bone-meal, frangipani, and old leathers. When they place their hand on mine, their flesh is warm. Strange how natural this feels, this configuration of phalanges and dermis. With my husband, buried now in the guts of our brood, it had always felt like a violation, even his most innocuous caress. "One question for one of my own."

I nod, letting go of the mask so I might lace our fingers together.

"You first."

I cup the plague doctor's chin with the hand I have free,

taking care to stroke the sutures ridging the flesh, and they laugh in easy reply.

"These," they ask.

They detach my grip—so gentle, so cautious of where and how our bodies fit—and place their fists on their lap, body slanted away, the long column of their frame held perfectly still. The plague doctor does not even breathe. "Did you ever wonder why I took an interest in your person? It is because we are not unlike, you and I. We are both *manufactured* beings."

Manufactured. Understanding frissons. With new eyes, I contemplate the variegation in their complexion, how some swathes of skin are infinitesimally lighter than their neighbour, how their fingers share no commonality in texture. No, we are not very different at all, even if one is fashioned with thread and dried sinew, the other cleaved and then conjugated by magic.

"My turn. What is your name?"

I breathe the cold, deep.

And I place the sound—a guttural exhalation made coherent by what little magic glitters still inside me—into the plague doctor's keeping.

⌒

Myths are full of lies.

This is not one of them.

Names are like selkie-skins, often carelessly attended, left in view of those who would misuse them. Utilized correctly, though, they can kill a man, can turn a girl to a thing of teeth and dead eyes, an appetite to devour worlds; can make infernos of maidens, phoenixes of bones who have been asleep for so long they've forgotten the shape of rage.

Names have so much power.

Enough even to hide a soul in the curl of a stranger's tongue.

~

"That is hard to pronounce."

I shrug. The language of the deepwaterbasal, marrow-deep—does not require air, or tongue, or even lips to mold. But their indignance—inflected in the rueful bend of their mouth, the restless way they carve furrows through their hair, over and over in nervous repetition—extracts a smile from me. I'd missed the plague doctor, I realize. My husband hoarded my pregnancy, its moments and movements, the waxing of my womb an aching minuet, choreographed to his amusements, his ambitions. I was permitted no company save for what he'd curated, no conversation but his.

"No matter. I—"

A shriek. Two boys explode from the woods, one in pursuit of the other. The former is taller, paler, whipcord-muscle beneath a mantling of fur. He holds an iron stake in one hand, the jut of polished metal rested against his hip. The tip is black.

His quarry is smaller, gangly as a puppet, barely more than gristle lashed to growing bones, and peculiarly naked despite the winter. He runs with his hand pressed to his belly, the flesh gashed open. Behind his palm, I see grey intestine, membrane bulging between the slats of his fingers. The snow blooms red beneath his feet, a splotching of color like bloodied tongues. Saliva wells in the room of my mouth.

The taller one leaps.

For the frame of a second, there is only silence, only the taiga holding its breath, only the firelight reflected against the wet of the stake as it thrusts through the gap between two ribs. A sharp intake of air as the stake burrows into organ matter. A scream gurgling through punctured lungs. They slam into the frozen soil, fur and gore and pasty flesh. Snow fountains.

The plague doctor is on their feet before I can react, shouting furiously, their hood shucked, their mask replaced. Their words churn, meaningless, in my ears. I am spellbound. I watch as one boy rises, triumphant, over the corpse of the other. He grins at me, his eyes jellyfish-light, the pupils swollen, before punching his stake into the air.

"The pig is dead!"

More baying from the forest. Four boys emerge, all dressed in deerleather, faces obscured beneath antlered skulls. Three of them carry torches, one a leather tarp that he drags across the ground. All four have knives.

They're quick but my plague doctor is quicker, leashing the murderer by his wrist before he can escape. A tug and then—*crack*. Bones separate beneath practiced hands, cartilage torquing apart. The boy howls his agony, chokes as the plague doctor secures him against their breast, his throat beneath their forearm, a sliver of polished metal balanced on the throb of his jugular.

"What are you *doing*?" the boy with the tarp demands. His

voice is fluting, castrato high. He can't be any more than nine, ten, too young to comprehend the danger his friend confronts. "Let Samson go!"

The others say nothing, only watch with eyes that burn gold in the dimming firelight.

"Your friend is a murderer," the plague doctor intones. "Worse yet, he's a trespasser. Where we come from, these things are sins."

A lie if ever there was one. But even if I had a voice with which to correct my companion, I would have said nothing. I bite down on my smile instead, straightening, aware of how I must look: transparent hair, translucent skin, lips red as arteries. Iridescent eyes, stained-glass oceans, so large that they are nearly alien, their breadth magnified by thick, sweeping lashes. With every hour that passes, every morsel of flesh to worm down my throat, I become closer to what I was, what I am: an inhuman thing wrenched from the maw of the sea.

And like dogs scenting danger, the boys oil away from me, warning humming in their throats. I grin and they almost bark.

"We didn't *murder* him," Samson hisses. "It's just a game!"

"I have been a physician for seventy-two years. I have walked the alleys of my murdered country, counted the bodies and set them to paper. Believe me when I say I *know* how to identify a corpse."

"But he *isn't* a corpse. That's just the pig's body."

The tiniest motion of the plague doctor's fingers, and the blade unseams Samson's flesh. Blood pearls along the polished steel. "I don't see the distinction."

"Look, we just need to get his bezoar and take it home. He'll be good as new once the saints fix him up!"

"A bezoar?" The anger drifts from the plague doctor's voice, and the space it abandons is soon tenanted by something else: a kind of horror, muslin-light.

"We've all been the pig before. Aren't I right, fellas?" says the boy with the tarp. The others nod enthusiastic agreement. "And we've all come out better for it. The saints make sure of it."

"Builds character," declares one of the silent ones, stockiest of the group, his voice already broken by adolescence.

"Let us take the bezoar back and we'll let Luke himself explain how okay this all is," Samson continues. "We got a deal?"

"I—" The plague doctor's composure flickers. They swallow and step back, freeing Samson from his incarceration. "What do you think?"

I dip my chin.

"Fine," says the plague doctor. "We'll come with you. But if you're lying, your lives shall be forfeit."

"Cor, you're cute. Like dying ever scared any of us." A flash of white teeth as Samson drops to a wide-kneed squat, his stake exchanged for a scalpel. His glee is palpable, but wholly benevolent. "You're going to be so surprised."

Even one-armed, the other useless from having been maimed by the plague doctor, Samson is dexterous. He cuts just beneath the dead boy's ribs, the blade tilted slightly upwards, and then down along the sides to carve out a flap. With care, he peels the meat back. Steam wafts from the ropey mass of entrails, green and grey and buttery fat. As we watch, Samson slides his fingers past the small intestine, his face contorted into a rictus, and carefully, so carefully, he extracts a lump of flesh the size of a goose egg.

"There," Samson declares, feline in his satisfaction. "We got him."

And to this, the plague doctor, their face starved of all expression, says nothing at all.

～

There is a reason the hunt is central to so many narratives.

For all that humanity professes to delighting in its own sophistication, it longs for simplicity, for when the world can be deboned into binaries: darkness and light, death and life, hunter and hunted.

It is this desire, perhaps, that drives so many to seek spouses among the inhuman and the immortal. Valkyries who cloak themselves in swan feathers. Long-throated crane wives, foreheads slashed with scarlet. Fox girls with bloody mouths and carnivore grins. Dryads, fairy women, the huldra with spines of gnarled bark. And mermaids, of course, hunger and glimmering scales, like nothing the air might ever produce and nothing the land could hope to keep.

～

They walk us through the taiga, the corpse dragging behind us, bound in ropes of lavender-stuffed hemp. Above, snow begins to seep between branches, silent as it falls, catching onto the fan of my collar, the black of the plague doctor's cape. The snowflakes do not melt. The plague doctor keeps pace beside me, my hand gloved in theirs, an affection we negotiate with careful glances, a smile paid in advance. Our horse shambles behind, incensed to be moving again. We will not ride it for fear the boys are leading us somewhere treacherous. Better we walk than risk the gelding breaking a limb. The horse slaps the air from its tail. For a time, it is the only sound we hear, that hiss of horsehair in motion, metered by the dirge of our footsteps and the breeze, ice-snarled and diamantine, like the breath of a dying hare.

But then the boys begin to sing, a gospel of endless vowels, consonants used only to demarcate where breath must be taken. The youngest carries his notes like they'll save him, cups them in cantatas of silver, while the others stalk his mordents like they're the death of them, their lean tenors glissading to baritones, to uneven bass. I look questioningly to the plague doctor, who'd taken again to wearing their mask.

At my gaze, they shrug: "Who knows?"

Some part of me does, I'm certain, for my heart strains in rhythm. But whatever secrets it has accreted, the organ will not share. We continue on until at last the pine and the aspen give way to cottages and flickering candlelight, silhouettes behind grubby windows, dirt roads and anemic gardens, a salty fragrance of woodsmoke and baking bread. Serviceable but spare, unremarkable as villages go. At least, it would have been were it not for one peculiarity.

Bodies, some already rotted to gristle, most mummified in frost, dangle from carelessly erected gallows. Fifteen in total and none with their lower halves intact. One—the oldest, I think—is nothing but chest and wilted spine.

"We're here," declares Samson, full of yearning.

I glance over as he unwraps whatever he'd excised from the dead boy's viscera: a bolus of broken-off teeth and snarled hairs, fingernails, caked dirt, curds of mummified grey, colored glass. Over it all, a lettering of fine blue veins, like an alphabet that only muscle can decode. It throbs in his grip, alive. He smiles at the bezoar before bellowing.

"Pig is back! Tell the saints!"

An answering chorus: "Dinner's ready! The saints are told!"

Teenagers flit from the doorways, girls and boys both, gaunt as jackals, their hair twined with bones and dried ixora, their cheeks finger-dotted with indigo. Whooping, they rush us, surround us. The horse rears, kicks hard at one, and his sternum folds in half. He tumbles to the accompaniment of his companions' laughter. Two pause to gather his concave-chested body away, red foam dribbling from a pouting lip, and as they turn a corner, I catch them kissing him, each to a cheek.

"Stay close." The plague doctor bares their knife and I bare my teeth, but no one takes notice, devouring Samson with their eyes, their panting attention. Even the dead ignore us, sockets black with accusation.

"Did it take long?"

"What did the prize look like?"

"Were you careful? When it was Luke's turn—"

And so on and so forth, a fumble of inanity, circling the exquisite question of a hunt, a kill: the what, the where, the how loud did he scream. Occasionally, one will stroke fingers across the dead boy's bezoar, their face shimmering with worship. Samson doles out his answers like some god freshly sleeved in integument, magnanimous, blessing his responses with an anointment of touch, the heel of his palm laid across their foreheads.

"Welcome back, children."

Beside me, the plague doctor stiffens.

It is a male voice that speaks, wine-dark, thick as syrup, drunk on its own percussions.

"Welcome."

"Welcome."

Two more voices follow in chorus, each a sliver of an octave higher than the last, each a beat slower, a susurrant madrigal like some deathbed hallucination. Three men emerge from the throng wearing matching hats, with matching gaits and wool-lined capes rippling behind. Even their masks—bauta with ornate trims, heavy and indelibly masculine—are identical, down to the filigreed beards. Bone overlaid with porcelain, seamed with gold and drips of ice-washed ruby, a tasseling of diamonds to accent the sharpness of their jaws. Antlers for one, curling horns for the other two.

One cocks his head. The other two repeat the motion.

"What did you bring us?"

"Bring us."

"Bring us."

Samson turns his gaze, stares at us like this is the first time he has borne witness to our presence. A frown etches itself between his eyes. The carrion smell of him—stomach juices, a pang of sweat, blood rusted beneath the nail bed—makes my mouth water again. The plague doctor's fingers, threaded with my own, spasm.

"Oh. Them," says Samson, noncommittal. "We found them while we were on the Hunt. The one in black thought I was a murderer, so I thought I'd bring 'em to you to explain the situation."

The men—physicians like my plague doctor, I imagine, what with the dry floral reek of them, their monochrome uniform, these saints of the children, these hallowed butchers—move closer still, no sound at all to their motions.

"I see."

"I see."

"I *see*."

"Can they watch while you fix up Luke?" Samson, the soul of flippancy, his bravado so close to breaking, swaggers up to the three, both palms cradling the bezoar. He sets it in their grip, steps back.

They do not answer, only turn, heaving their secrets behind them.

⌒

Certain stories are recounted so many times that they become parched of meaning, stories like those concerning the girl and her wolf in the woods, the cinder-smudged princess, the monstrous beauty who vomits pearls with every sob.

Others, however, are kept from taverns and wine-warmed conversations, catalogued but rarely recited. Complicated stories with no easy ending, stories that remind us karmic debt is a contrivance of despair, that there is nothing fair or sweet about this world.

The tale of how some children played slaughtering together is one of them.

The story of the three army surgeons is another.

～

We are led to a hovel built so small that my plague doctor must duck beneath its entrance. Inside, it is warm and fragrant. The ribs of roof expand to a steepled point, its rungs lush with nooses strung with drying herbs: dill, tarragon, purple opal basil, savory, wreaths of smoked black garlic. As for the furnishings, they are ascetic: a bed of sweet-smelling hay with a threadbare duvet; a fireplace; a table, two chairs; a single cabinet to hold whatever possessions we might have.

There are signs that someone else might have lived here, might have been evicted to create space for us. Chewed-up chicken bones kicked into the corners. A cup of tea on the table, half-drunk. Some books. I pick up the closest volume, flip through the pages to where the text has been dog-eared, run a finger through the paragraphs, the childish handwriting.

"What's this?" The plague doctor pads up behind me, their chin on my shoulder.

A bible, I would have said had I a tongue to shape the words, not a brief wag of muscle. A scripture. A palimpsest improvised from a religion older, crueler, bloodier than even what was venerated in my husband's kingdom. An ancient story retold as a game to waste the winter with, a wager as antiquated and cold as the ocean's deep. I turn the page. Drawings populate the margins, more sophisticated than the calligraphy. Images of the three men, captured from every angle, always with their masks, their dense fur cloaks.

"You know," remarks my plague doctor. "I'd expected them to set themselves up as kings. But as gods? That seems a bit arrogant even for them. Oh, well." A taut, ugly laugh.

They sit themselves on the bed, their hat anchored against their heart. I stare at them, wordless, expectant. But the plague doctor reveals nothing, only sheds their mask so I might regard the pensiveness that has possessed them. If I had the voice for such a thing, I might have whispered then that they were beautiful, deified in the firelight, with their cheekbones carved for killing, their hair a halo of curling inks.

Instead, I say nothing.

"Do your people believe in an afterlife?" They pluck tufts of straw from beneath them, grimacing.

I shake my head. What need is there for such platitudes when you are born to yourself time and again? Like a story, we are the summation of our incarnations, a spirit refracted through a billion lives. We are our pasts, our futures, tethered by the flavor of our sisters' flesh.

"Ours do." A smile, or something like a smile, invents itself upon their lips. "Even though no one has ever discovered any proof that we are more than meat and bone, humans continue to hold on to the belief that some part of us will persist after our deaths. The unscrupulous have built an entire industry on this."

I glide towards the plague doctor, shrugging free of my furs as

I do, and stop inches from their knees, my hands outstretched. They nuzzle their jaw into my hands, allow my fingers to cinch about their skull. I could snap their neck, dislocate the vertebrae stacked upon each other, sever the blood flow. They know this. I do too. Nonetheless, they place their faith and their breakable flesh in my fingers, eyes closed.

"But they are not all charlatans." The plague doctor does not kiss my skin, does not move to restrain me, does not do anything but rest their cheek in my grasp, its stitching rough against my palm. "There were three—surgeons, I suppose you could call them. They were better than the rest of them. They understood how one might lengthen the life of another, might prolong the function of a failing body by exchanging old parts for new. Eventually, they grew more curious. Could you assemble a new life from nothing but debris?"

Their smile erodes. Their voice fades.

"You would be amazed by what you can do when you have faith, when you know how to commoditize someone else's faith, when you know the trick of words like *hold on* and *tomorrow*. I—"

The door opens, admitting the winter and a stranger's flickering silhouette. The figure outside our doorway is small-boned and long-haired, clad in the barest of wools, a fox's carcass around their throat. They shiver, bones chattering.

"They're asking for you." A high, piping voice. What I imagine my sister-daughters might have wielded had they been born human, rosy-cheeked and plump. The sounds of the village swell to a fever, drumbeats metered by youthful voices.

"Was this yours?" says the plague doctor, and they gesture

with a hand, the graceful parabola of the motion encompassing the room at large.

The girl says nothing, only clenches her jaw.

"So very like them. To take and redistribute what never belonged to them," the plague doctor murmurs bitterly, untangling themself from my fingers to rise in a murmur of onyx fabric. I follow behind, wordless, watchful.

~

They were always men, those itinerant storytellers, for the bitter winding roads—bandit-swollen, lord-haunted—were and, for all that I might wish otherwise, will likely always be unkind to women. I remember the first of them to arrive in the court. He was lithe, circumspect in conduct. His coat was wrinkled. He wore a cravat around an untidy collar and had untidy curls that fluffed along his ears. The maidservants called him unhandsome, but he was kind to me and for that, I adored him.

"You remind me of me," he told me once, sadly and quietly. Dusk had glazed the chamber in glowing indigo, gilded the chairs, the hulking cinnabar armoire, its surface engraved with vignettes of primordial birth. I could smell my evening's repast: something choking with cream, fresh vanilla pods, a hint of citrus. "Trapped."

In response, I shrugged and wrote him another koan to decrypt, this one pertinent to the rites of ceremonial fratricide. Later, I'd learn of the palimpsest he'd made from my stories, how he told the world that a mermaid, should she prove virtuous enough, may hope to transform into a daughter of air. Of all the men who have mistold my history, I resent him least. Like me, he stood anchored in gilded chains, throat and wrists collared by another's presumptions, breath beaten to gasps by a world that permits only a single direction: forward and away from our heart's desire.

He was not quite wrong, but he certainly was not right.

~

There is a body on a pyre of dried reeds, the leaves wefted with lilies and out-of-season poppies, like rosaries of fresh blood; jasmine and sprigs of drooping wisteria, frangipani like petals of meringue, harvests of sweet alyssum. The saccharine headiness of them nearly disguises the odor of the carcass, the formaldehyde in which its viscera has been steeped.

Around the bier, the children of the village have gathered on their knees, rocking to a droning hymn that they pass from throat to throat. The three surgeons stand silent.

I do not recognize the corpse until we've drawn close enough for touch, its face obscured beneath a thin haze of golden hair. Someone had butterflied Luke's torso, pinned the flaps of skin to its sides with stalks of glass, trapped his wrists and his ankles in coils of burlap. The cuts are exact; no wasted incisions, a masterpiece of the medical abattoir.

Carefully, I smooth a hand across Luke's brow, parting the hair from his features. His expression is gentle, beatific, without the scarring that death sometimes inflicts. I had expected a rictus. Pain. It isn't until my fingers find the stitching—the finest sutures, so exquisitely delicate that they may as well be illusionary—that I understand why.

"Welcome."

"Welcome."

"Welcome."

"You're just in time." The doctors arrange themselves on the right of the body, every motion matched and mirrored, Luke's bezoar transferred from hand to hand, before it is at last installed in the abdominal cavity, just above the rise of the pelvic bone.

"In time."

"In time."

Cogs come next, bronze in the firelight. Toothed discs, spirals of wire. "A new round is to begin. When Luke reawakens, he will play the role of the butcher, and another will be chosen as the pig. Such is the game that we play, the exercise that we must perform to ready the body."

"Butcher."

"*Pig.*"

The last is a whisper, ravenous.

One of the doctors crooks a hand and a boy—I remember him from the taiga, the one with a soaring voice of crystal— rises to provide access to an open jar, the container massive enough that he must clutch it with both arms. Inside, coils of intestine, succulent and redolent of brine. About two feet of the winding organ is meticulously removed. The rest is returned to salt water. The same is done with a glossy slab of liver, a stomach, rinds of muscle still on the bone: everything is measured, mapped to the millimeter, before a segment is taken and joined to Luke's extant viscera.

Not once do the three surgeons pause or falter, knives and thread and needle flashing, a life cohering beneath their long fingers. At some indeterminable interval between then and tomorrow, Luke swallows a ragged breath. His lungs—pale, smooth pink, wisping steam—expand.

And he *screams*.

With his eyes rolled back. With his body convulsing in time with every paroxysm of noise. With the terror of the dead coerced back into its carcass, and the choking knowledge that comes after: now it must teach the heart to beat, the blood to run, the body to breathe when before there had only been the dirt, the quiet.

This is nothing clean about this, nothing that merits celebration, nothing *willing*, no agreement on the part of the resurrected boy. I twitch away from the sight of him spasming against his restraints. His peers do not share my repulsion. They roar up from their obeisances, howling, exulting in the debacle they've witnessed. When Samson turns to us, his eyes are fanatic-bright.

"See?" His grin is a knife. "Told you they'd make Luke good as new."

To their credit, the doctors do not indulge in their edification and focus instead on the completion of their task. As Luke thrashes in agony, one moves to pin him down by the shoulders, while another secures his ankles. The third works rapidly, lacing the boy's dermis together with filaments that are almost invisible in the firelight.

Through it all, Luke continues to scream and scream; his lungs swollen against his ribs.

"What have they *done?*" my plague doctor moans. I find their hand and slot my fingers between theirs, find them trembling, their pulse juddering in its veins. "What have they done," they repeat. "What have they done. What have they done."

I squeeze their hand as the children's saints begin to speak.

"You see?"

"You see."

"You see."

"I see—" begins my plague doctor, the words hoarse. "—three men who have participated in the torture of a poor child. First, you catalyze his murder and *now?* After he has at last fled this wretched earth, you drag him back, and *bind* him to steel and sinew."

"Every newborn screams when they first emerge into this world." They sigh together, and there is something petulant about the acoustics of their retort, a churlishness that pricks. "This is no different."

"You say this"—a baring of teeth as the plague doctor's voice crescendos—"you say this as men who have never practiced their art on themselves. You say this as men who have never known pain, who cannot know pain. You say this—"

A stillness fits its maw around the crackling of the torches, the wind as it laces cold around the village, a moaning nearly too low to hear. Sensing blood in the wind, the crowd stills, their lambent gaze turned to the surgeons, expectant.

They transmit a look among themselves, heads moving like

clockwork sparrows, the barest motions. "We would not do unto others what we have not done to ourselves. This pain—"

"This pain."

"This pain."

"—is transitory, a signal of a body that is learning to change, to better itself. When you have become like us, when you have *transcended,* there will be nothing but beauty. But we understand your lack of trust. For you, we will prove ourselves again." An inflection of the hand, repeated in triplicate. "You will see."

~

This is the spectacle we witness:

For the first act, the first doctor severs his hand at the wrist: a smooth descent of a bone saw, a tensing and uncurling of muscles in the dominant grip. No blood seeps from the resultant stump, only a paste-like substance: dark, sweet-smelling.

For the second, the next doctor uses spoons of polished ivory, their stems traced with brass, to commit self-enucleation. The optic nerves he crops with pearl-handled scissors, and the assembly claps at his sightless efficiency.

For the coda of this performance, the last doctor excises his own heart. A complicated exercise requiring the foreshortening of the ribs and a movement of the lungs, the trachea, the digestive tract at its nascence. Arteries are pinioned, veins clipped, their contents rerouted. Where to, I couldn't begin to tell you, but the art of the doctor is such that he continues to breathe, continues to work without regard for the vanished organ.

When he is done, the trifecta of body parts is set on a tray of obsidian and lofted by a girl with hair like a spill of oil.

"Do you see now?" the three cry in unison, voices bolstered by the paeans of their disciples, messianic in their mutilation. In that moment, they are nothing if not mythic, nothing if not gods of this small place, this snow-swallowed taiga. "Do you not *see*?"

My plague doctor, of course, says nothing at all.

II

The Second Night

In the minutes before dawn arrives, when the indigo horizon has only just begun to bleed, a reddish-gold seeping between the cracks in the mountain line, I slip from the hovel and pad towards a hut alcoved by the trees.

I can smell them. The eyes, the heart, the amputated hand. A sour-sweetness, faintly chemical, as though of roses beginning to ferment, underscored by a wash of roasted marrow, rich fat. And magic too. Fecund, familiar.

I push the door and a slant of light baptizes the dark, limns the rosewood shelves and their occupants in cobalt, the bottles thick with offal. But they are not what I am here for. I find what I'm looking for on an oval of black stone. Though unprotected, no frost has touched them. The heart, in particular, is unusually warm.

The three surgeons had described these parts as vestigial, no more important than a twist of hair, or the skin scraped from the back of a knee. This, they said, was an example of the providence that they've vowed to share, the benediction that awaits those who would persevere, would permit themselves to suffer. Heaven can only be bridged by agony, they cried.

One day soon, there wouldn't even be need for that. One day, the surgeons whispered, there would be no reason to fear mortality. If only the faithful endure. After all, *look*: have they not detached the very hand from one, removed the eyes from another, exhumed the heart from the third? Do they not stand among their acolytes, not only alive but *vigorous*? Was this not proof enough of numinosity?

So I eat them, the detritus they've left behind.

I pop the eyes into my mouth first. They are almost ephemeral, tasting of ice and salted limes. The hand is a more complicated flavor: gingery, unctuous, the phalanges crunching like pork crackling beneath my teeth. And the heart—no pang of metal or rotting tissue here, but something exponentially more divine, its potent sapidity recalling my first memory of being conscious, and aware of my bathyal womb.

As I lick the surface clean of its juices, I wonder if my plague doctor would object to what I've done, or if they'd laugh. Either way, the surgeons *had* said they have no use for these.

～

"We should leave."

I lave my tongue across my teeth, savoring their calcium flavor, the few strings of tissue caught between. How I'd missed this, longed for this: taste in its orchestral complexity, every flavor note relayed without exception. My voice—I do not recognize the chords, its abraded cadence, but the shape of it? Still enough of mine that I ache at its echoes. The flesh of the surgeons is more restorative even than the ambitions of my hope. Whatever else they are, whatever else they might represent, they are good meat, nonetheless.

"You can talk." The plague doctor sits up straight. It is strange to see them without their usual regalia, their robes strung on a line outside the open window. Instead of black, they now wear alkaline white, their vestments not unlike what a travelling monk might don: close-fitted with asymmetrical paneling, the collar high enough to kiss their lower lip. Drenched in the morning sunlight, their copper skin almost glows. "I'd always thought—"

"That I was possessed by a drowning hunger for the sun and as such, chose to surrender my voice for a chance to have the sun warm my shoulders? That I loved him, my husband, with such fury, that I laid everything I was at his feet like a dowry? No. Lies, all of them. Myths to make my captivity more palatable. He cut out my tongue and fed the pieces to me." I touch fingertips to my throat. Something about my repast had been exceptionally curative. "But later, we can sift through the falsehoods. For now, we need to leave."

"What did—" The question catches between their teeth, a hissed intake of breath. "Oh."

I smile. "They said these things were extraneous."

The plague doctor angles a strange look, eyes liquid. As they rake fingers through coal-dark curls, an epiphany articulates itself: all these years and not once have they offered the use of their name. They sigh. "You're surprisingly eloquent."

"When you do not have the option for conversation, there arises a wealth of time for personal instruction." I fold myself into the opposite chair, a smile budding. My voice rasps and scratches, rusted by the silence, but it is mine, still mine. "Let us be gone."

"We can't."

"Why?"

"The children—" Their voice knots itself in old memories, dies before it can be born. That crack in their facade, the one I'd glimpsed in the woods, I see it dilate again and a drop of terror pitches into their expression. In that moment, they are young, haunted, eminently breakable.

I glance at the window. No one else has arisen yet. No one save our missing host, I suppose, ill-fitting as the description might be. After all, the word implicates some measure of consensuality, and I suspect her agreement was never courted. Certainly, her behavior suggested as much. Late into the previous night, after the last torch had burned itself black, the girl who'd first summoned us—fox-haired, scrawny—entered to nest beside the dwindling fire. She wouldn't speak to us, would only glare from between matted bangs, glowering as the plague doctor ransacked her notes.

"You want to free them."

"That would be presumptuous." Wryness winds itself through their voice. The plague doctor rises, paces to the windowsill where their mask rests drying, the monk's cloth of their garments whispering hoarse secrets. "I want them to free themselves."

"Why?"

"Did you not see what they did to the poor boy? No child should live through an eternity of that. Trust me. I've spent enough time under those curious hands to—"

The plague doctor falls silent.

Ah, I think.

"The surgeons. They're the ones who made you, weren't they?"

They say nothing. I read instead the answer in the tension lines of their mouth, their opaque gaze, the blanched knobs of their knuckles as they crumple the fabric of their robes into a trembling hand.

"Whatever the case," I say, gentle. "I suspect that your makers—"

They tense at the word.

"—will not take kindly to what I have done. Forget what their disciples might do, regardless of whether their saints survive." I graze their shoulder blade with a touch and say, not unkindly, "We should leave. Now."

A spill of voices. Too late, then. I turn as the door gapes open, soundless, and a boy slips through, his face unfamiliar. Today, there are no bones wefted in the hair, no paint on soft cheeks; a fresh-scrubbed angelicness is in residence instead. He smiles, a crack between his incisors. "You two hungry? The saints are asking to have breakfast with you."

The plague doctor dons their mask, lips thinned beneath the sloping dark.

"Show the way."

The boy grins, effulgent. He prances forward, never once looking behind, already confident that where he marches, others must follow. We exchange another look, the plague doctor and I. With a slanting of their hand, they gesture me closer, close enough to mantle me with furs scavenged from our little quarters: squirrel skins, rabbit hides, delicate as eyelashes. The ritualism of my dressing, the attention they invest in the act, every motion elegiac, elegant; it proposes the presence of an unconsummated tenderness, something more profound than camaraderie.

I tilt my cheek, feel their breath puff against my flesh, and there is the sense of timelines fractalizing. In some other world, somewhere, perhaps they kiss me: lightly, feverishly, with the emphasis of desperation, with hesitation, with passion requited.

Here, they only chuckle and pull away. The two of us move in simpatico, keeping time with each other, always parallel, dark and light and the smell of plasma from my clandestine repast cooling on my fingertips. We are led to a banquet table, clumsily ornamented. Four figureheads, one to each leg, their arms raised to support the wood. The faces are hideous: gashes for the eyes and mouth, the jaws swollen to tumors.

The three surgeons slouch in their thrones, hats crowned with red poppies and glistening grey thorns, willow-branch braids. Today, the three wear pantalone half-masks, enamel-crusted leather in the pigments of violent death. A gluttonous amount of food—berries, black as bruising; figs; roasted poultry;

fried capers; cheeses pungent with salt—lies piled in front of them, untouched. Around them, the children cluster. There are only two little stools opposite where the surgeons sit like idols on their carved wooden thrones.

The plague doctor makes them wait. They smooth down both sleeves, one after another, adjusting the glide of creamy fabric before they straighten, stride forward. I watch as I always have: watch, wait, teeth demurely withheld.

"Discipline by deprivation, then?" A trimming of venom in their smooth contralto, candid.

"Yes," says one.

"Yes."

"You seem—" The third surgeon—the one with the tenor, the one who had gouged out his eyes—sighs and leans forward, shoulders scissored back. His mask is a drowned man's blue, and his gaze, restored somehow, whole again, is the color of medusae washed to shore, all turgid transparence and shuddering villi. I've seen eyes like those. Out in the taiga where everything was ice and nothing was as pale as one triumphant glare, steam uncurling beneath bared teeth. "—so *very* familiar."

"When you've seen one plague doctor, you've seen them all. I—" The plague doctor cants a look at the silent children. "Where is Samson?"

"Elsewhere."

"Indisposed."

"Away doing *great* things," says the third who sighs then, jellyfish eyes drowsy. "You *know* how children are."

Something throbs through the plague doctor, minute paroxysms most visible in the fingers. Was that recognition? An invocation of trauma past? By *away*, I wonder if the surgeons mean dead, his youth cannibalized. I wonder if his remains have been distributed among them, segregated by value, with better jars for better specimens. Is *his* bezoar somewhere, dreaming of renascence? My plague doctor exhales, slow, and I glide up beside them, shoulder fitted against theirs, a comfort offered.

"You'll have to teach me that trick," says my plague doctor, one corner of their mouth raised, their gaze languid as it moves to rest upon the surgeon who had enucleated himself. "Nothing of my research has revealed how to adjust the color of the iris. And do not think to be coy, sir. I am excellent at detail and I know the color of your eyes today is not the same as what it was before."

A beat.

"They look just like Samson's," says the plague doctor, and there is enough venom in their voice to boil the breath from a dynasty.

"Stay." One steeples his gloved hands, but I see what he's trying to hide beneath the silk. In the circlet of bare flesh between where the gloves end and his sleeves begin: a subtle patterning under the skin, as though of string cabled through sinew, holding together muscles until fresh nerves can take root. This then is the nature of their immortality: a cruel parasitism, worse than the hunger of the hunt and its teeth. "And we will."

"Stay."

"Stay."

"We would, but we need to feed the horse," the plague doctor drawls, fingers circling my wrist. I do not resist when they pull me away. The surgeons say nothing, the children say even less.

～

"This is your fault," they say without accusation, only a dry-mouthed, shambolic despair. The plague doctor wrings their hands as they pace along the frozen riverbank. Across the way, a lynx is testing the ice with too-wide paws, ears bent low, its tawny reflection abstracted by the rime.

"The fact they killed Samson?"

The plague doctor flinches. "Must you put it so bluntly?"

"I cannot change what I am." I sit beside our horse, the animal tethered to an ancient cedar, the puzzle of its dry, dead boughs adorned with ribbons chewed ragged by the passing seasons. I am surprised that the skittish beast tolerates me so well. Already, my mount has taken one life since our journey together began, collapsing that poor boy's sternum like bird bones between my teeth. But me, the equine indulges with its indifference, even the occasional nuzzle.

"I forget that your kind are so *practical*."

If the remark was intended as insult, it finds no crack in my psyche. The truth liberates; it cannot cripple or maul, cannot injure, not unless one declares themselves its apostate. I shrug, one-shouldered. The abyss does not leave much room for niceties. "A mermaid—"

"Are the rumors true then? Are you all female? Do you—"
Even in an hour of crisis, one's nature is difficult to refute. The

plague doctor ceases their listless patrol, widens their eyes, curiosity unfurling the lengthy comma of their spine.

I merely gaze at them in return, impassive.

"My apologies." They palm the back of their neck. "That was unnecessary."

I say nothing. The ice breaks beneath the lynx, gobbles it whole; the cat doesn't even have opportunity to scream, only vanishes beneath the black water, a gasp of gold and then nothing at all. The plague doctor doesn't take notice, frozen in their ruminations.

"We should leave," I whisper, after the silence has had time to steep, a fog breathing across the river.

"We can't. I told you," the plague doctor replies rigidly, as though compelled by rote. "Well. *You* can. I won't stop you. But I have to stay. I can't—" They stiffen. "I can't."

I fit a burlap morral—while we slept, someone'd filled it with hay, cabbage, wilted baby's breath—around the horse's skull and pat its flank. It rises, grumbling into its feed. "You cannot save everyone. You know that."

"I do."

Between us stretches the recollection of a massacre, the bodies stacked shoulders-deep, mostly eaten, the sun red, and the sky sloughing soot and skin. An entire country, ingested in days. Not for the first time, I wonder why they tolerate my presence. After all, I am the distillation of their failure, the mother of the plague they could not stop. They stare at me, loss in their expression.

"So let us leave," I say, gentler than before, different words crowding my lungs, the ghosts of a separate life. "There is nothing for us here."

THE SALT GROWS HEAVY

They sigh. "I cannot."

"Clearly, your makers—"

"Do not call them that."

"Creators, then. Gods. What would you prefer I call them?" My tone is measured, modulated, still as the water in a corpse's lungs. "You are their offspring, are you not? Would you prefer I call them your parents? I can."

"Stop." The plague doctor kneads the bridge of their nose. A muscle beneath their eye quivers.

"I tire of this. I understand your Hippocratic impulse for compassion, but you are too late. These children are already like you. Every last one of them, I'm certain. And they relish this existence. Can you not see that? You may have no love for your makers—"

"I said *stop*."

"—but these children *worship* the surgeons. Who are you trying to save? Really? Them, or some image of your juvenile self that you've preserved through the years?"

"Go." The word unwraps into a moan. Every sentence that follows is snapped. Every syllable is brittle as old bone. "I promised you nothing. I vowed nothing. I swore no oath of service. If what you desire is to leave? *Leave.* I don't understand your insistence that I follow. We owe each other nothi—"

"I owe you the loyalty of being the only other one."

"Ha." An expulsion of air, sharp and short, as though they'd endured the impact of a fist. The plague doctor sways and buries their face in their palms, shoulders quivering. The laugh that seeps from between their fingers is a lunatic noise, untethered to decorum or rhythm. It is all agony, the sound, like the hitching gasps of a dying child. "You're absolutely right. We are but distorted mirrors of one another. Murderer and murdered, butcher and doctor."

A ragged breath, filtered through clenched teeth.

"You are *probably* right. It is—" Always a pause before the word is spoken, always a tremor in its lilt. They drop their hands, straighten. "—*probably* too late for some. For most, even. It is *probably* a foolish idea . . . but yet. I remember *being* them, you understand? And I remember what followed. I was so young then. I—you are a mother. Surely, you must understand where I am coming from. Do you not care that they are children?"

"No." I think of the lynx beneath the river, its veins crystallizing. Of Luke on his bier, newborn and screaming, the wet pink of his lungs like the ruined stub of a tongue hidden behind a smile. Of my daughters, suckling the marrow from their father's kingdom, growing stronger by the hour. "Like everything else, they are only meat."

～

"Perhaps, we could simply kill them in their sleep."

The plague doctor crooks a humorless smile. "Martyrs are more powerful than gods."

The village is awake. It bustles with music, off-key and playful. Children, no more than eight or nine in age, drag buckets from the outhouses, while others boil water, fillet root vegetables, defeather poultry, wash, sweep, mop, and otherwise attend to the myriad drudgeries of a pastoral existence. As for the older denizens: girls, rangy from neglect, their hair plaited into single braids, hack at the ice-crusted earth. Grim-faced boys claw at the tilled soil with their fingernails, sowing—

Bones.

Femurs like corn stalks, slender tibias, knucklebones they carefully pat into the moist loam. But it is the fecundity of the land that surprises me, not its morbid harvest. Under the snow, the dirt is rich and dark, looking like something you might grasp in the summer, soft enough to crumble between the fingers.

Beside me, the plague doctor's steps stutter to a pause. "What *is* this? I've never seen bones planted in the soil like such."

"It's for the Witch Bride," a familiar voice intones, polite and petulant. I look down to where the girl stands, defiant, the zenith of her head barely grazing the circumference of the plague doctor's shoulder. Unlike her peers, she wears her tresses in a topknot, the carmine strands oiled to a sheen. Her garments are androgynous, practical: tan blouse, leather doublet, breeches without a stitch of ornamentation, high boots, and an overcoat cinched at narrow hip bones.

I know the name. No one in my husband's kingdom did not. It was rumored that she was the downfall of that distant principality, a tepid marsh without historic importance, its only economy a trade in the hides of small mammals. It was rumored that she had no heart and thus had to steal the king's own organ, that she was a bone-wight, cruel, a lie accoutred in stolen flesh, that she was hungry, bitter, resentful of her spouse's sweet son.

It is always interesting to see how often women are described as ravenous when it is the men who, without exception, take without thought of compensation.

I smile at the girl and stoop so that we are eye to eye. "Why would she want a harvest of bones?"

"Don't know. They say she's building a new kingdom. Could be she's starting her own religion. I hear that she's been calling the bones back from the grave." Her pale brow rucks further. The bridge of her nose is sunburned, peeling, and her lips are flaked with dry skin. She scratches at her jaw. "None of your business, anyway."

"No, but nothing of what you're doing is labor a child should worry about," says the plague doctor.

I smile, careful not to expose my teeth. "Where is Samson?"

"Away. Like the saints said." Resentment fruits in her expression, a bitter crop. "I'd appreciate that you don't ask them any more questions on the subject."

"Why is that?" The plague doctor speaks, voice languorous. But I am learning to recognize its nuances, to identify performativity in their address.

"None of your business *either*."

"Fine." A sigh that ends with a sharp clack of molars, the plague doctor's manner turns impatient. Whatever poise they once possessed, it is gone now, pulped to an aftertaste. I straighten as they speak, hands vanished into my sleeves. "Can you at least attend to the horse?"

"Sure." The girl takes the proffered reins. For all their difference in stature, she exhibits no fear of the gelding, only that precocious surliness unique to youth. Both the plague doctor and I are silent as we watch the two depart, one clopping docilely behind the other. No one raises their attention from their labor to greet them. The children work without halt, breath crisping in the air.

Then at last:

"What now?"

The plague doctor pivots, raises themself slightly on the arch of a heel as they lean in, their voice warm against the skin of my ear. There is a grin in their next words, a texturing of teeth bared, feral. "How do you kill any religion? You convince its flock that their shepherds are wolves."

"And how do you plan to do that?"

"We find a Judas goat."

〜

We find Luke by a pond at the back of the village, kneeling before a stone shrine. It sits canopied beneath ice-beaded brambles, a single candle guttering at its heart. Its architecture is not wholly alien. Somewhere in my husband's library, I've glimpsed that gabled roof, the ligature of serpents; only larger, more elaborate in composition, with masonry whorled with creeping vines. A sight removed from the taiga and the terrain that the cold has annexed. I wonder: how would something like this find its way here?

Someone had brought offerings in obsidian plates, the black surface veined with gold. Nothing complicated: fresh bread, cured meats, a winter's repast. I sink onto the earth behind Luke, while the plague doctor remains standing. A breeze drags the scent of salt and woodsmoke, tannic acids and animal musk.

"What do you want?" Luke's voice is raw, low, hoarse from screaming. He slants a rheumatic gaze over his shoulder, mouth pulled into a line, and I see: pink muscle ribboning from his chin to his throat, an imperfection in the set of his eyes. The left—pellucid grey, almost without fault, only the tiniest fissuring—does not fit quite right in its socket. He blinks, the motion reptilian, right eye more sluggish than its counterpart.

"We've come to pay our respects," my plague doctor intones.

"Well, sod off."

Luke is thin as the turn of the waning moon, wrist bones protruding against waxy skin. His blond hair has been tonsured. On his bare scalp, a Vitruvian diagram in blue ink; some treatise on anatomy, perhaps, or a nautical chart with which sailors might sail the arteries of a leviathan.

"We apologize if we're overstepping," I begin. "Your makers—"

He flinches at the word the way my plague doctor does, and I know then that I have him. Like a fisherman, I am patient. I lower my timbre, adjust the intonation for sweetness, and watch as Luke works the hook inside his throat, shuddering with every gulp. "Your masters? Would you prefer that word?"

"T-the saints." He sags, finally relenting. "We call them the saints."

"The saints." I wind my tongue around the word, savor it. "Your saints told us little about what we may or may not do. We don't mean to offend."

When he does not reply:

"Does it hurt?" I cup my hand around his shoulder, fingers mapped to his clavicle.

Luke moans at the contact, like something broken-backed and dying. "Only a little," he whispers. "Only a little. A small thing, a small pain compared to the reward. I believe—"

"I can help stop the pain." A rustle of footsteps, heavy fabrics shifting and settling. The plague doctor interrupts. I withdraw. Their tone is gentle, tender even. "You don't have to suffer like this."

"The saints—"

"They don't have to know." Seduction at its most austere, an appeal to the simplest desire: survival. "Let me at least see what they've done, Luke. A look. That is all I ask. I will not make a single cut. Not unless you tell me to."

"Yes." So very soft, the tired answer. So very frightened.

I look to the tree line where the pines stand like a tribunal in judgment. Sunlight breaks itself upon their branches, and the world beneath them is stark, no color at all, a chiaroscuro of midnight and salt. I tilt my head. Between the roots, there are graves, I realize, planted so close to the trees that there can be no mistaking the purpose. What better use is there for the rotting tenement of the soul than as sustenance for new life, life that'd linger longer after history has been digested by moths and mold? Meat may be mulch when left for long enough.

Such a provident, unsentimental decision. Surely, one made by the surgeons, the saints of this strange place.

"Do they do this often?"

I blink, retrain my attention onto Luke and the plague doctor. They'd convinced the boy to partially disrobe, divulging shoulder blade and vertebrae. His back is a codex of mismatched dermis: dusk-dark, ivory, shades of red-gold bronze.

The stitching is sloppy, wide and uneven, performed with rough hessian thread instead of catgut.

"Only when we come back. The saints say it's to make us stronger for the next time."

"Shoddy work," the plague doctor remarks, perfunctory. They sit cross-legged behind Luke, tools and opened vials fanned out around them, a miasma of prophylactics souring the cold. With care, the plague doctor removes a scroll of pale vellum from a satchel, unfurls the sheet, makes cuts lengthwise. "If—"

I almost do not hear the words that follow. "They take things too."

"What things?" Their timbre is clinical, without unnecessary inflection. The plague doctor dips a scalpel in a bottle, wipes the flat of the blade along Luke's scapula, the latter's skin pimpling at the contact. "If you permit me, I can ease some of your discomfort. Muscle is not intended to be exposed like this. And the stitching"—a tsking noise—"is *appalling*."

"Yes."

A flick of the wrist. Light darts along sterilized steel. Thread unravels; the first loop comes apart. Steadily, the plague doctor descends the rung of sutures, daubing the places they pass with an astringent-smelling paste; citrus and cyanide, a tinting of caladium, foxglove in equal measure. Slowly, skin is exuviated, unwrapped in strips.

Through it all, Luke says nothing, emits no sound, only shudders and quakes. Perhaps from the cold, or perhaps the pain, or perhaps this show of compassion, however utilitarian its presentation.

"What did they take from you, Luke?" The plague doctor is efficient, methodical. Their stitching is evanescent. You'd miss it if you didn't know where to look. I recognize the smell of the string they've used: goat intestine shaved into fibers, cured and knitted together. In time, it will disintegrate, absorb into flesh, and the worst that Luke will endure is a stutter of scars.

"A half of my liver," he says, almost ashamed. "A kidney. Skin—"

"That much is evident."

A fluttering laugh. "They put some back."

I pick a coil of sloughed dermis from the snow and begin to gnaw on an end. The skin tastes musty, parchment-like. "Was that your punishment? For being caught?"

Killed, I almost say instead. *Would* have said were it not for the look in his eyes, his stare, the way he begins to shake, as though his skeleton might unlatch, separate into verses and phrases of hurt.

I hesitate. "You needn't tell me."

His tongue, small and pale, makes a circuit of his lips. "No, no. It's alright. The saints—they say fear is one of our two teachers. That if we want to, *ah*"—a hiss, as fresh skin is transposed onto trembling meat—"ascend, we must know what it is like to be hunted, *afraid*. The pig always dies. It has to."

"Why?" asks the plague doctor

"Because there must always be a beginning and an end."

The plague doctor vents their displeasure, a thrumming deep in the grooves of their chest. "Strange words from men hoping to capture immortality in a bottle. Tell me: is your joy sweeter for your knowledge of what it is like to die? Do you enjoy every sunset better? Or does it stain you, follow like the whisper of a nightmare that will not end with your waking? A whipped dog is not happy to see its owner, it is merely counting the hours until the next torment."

"The saints—" Defiance in the yaw of the words, his voice pitched high and quick. But Luke's protest is reflexive, without conviction.

"The saints don't know everything," says my companion.

"They *promised*."

"They lie."

~

We left him with a bottle of the poultice that my plague doctor had used. Enough, they'd said, to survive him a week and four nights. More, if he could stand to ration himself. The substrate dispensed chemical ecstasy, orgasmic yet knifelike.

"Don't drink it, though." The plague doctor had chuckled, the noise like an ice floe riving beneath small paws. "You'll die and there'd be nothing that your saints can do about it. There'd be nothing left of you but a silhouette on the ground."

For the first time since I'd known him, Luke looked happy.

~

"It has been a day, at least, since you've eaten."

The plague doctor slows, smiles, their natural inimicality softened for the pivot of a second. "You *care*."

When I commit nothing in answer, having no want to either

reassure or reprimand, they laugh, basal and heady. The woods grow thick here, along the hem of the village where it swells widest. Cedar and aspen, pine and white spruce, bent together in conspiracy. Under the eaves of their branches, the plague doctor's face turns strange, honeycombed by harsh shadow.

"Food is an indulgence, not a necessity. The bezoar requires no tending." They walk fingers to the nadir of a pelvic bone, press in. A sigh seeps. "It is the only part of me that is left, you know?"

I advance, a darting half step forward, so I am close enough that I can feel the heat from their skin. The plague doctor tips their chin and grips my hand, guides my fingers down to where their bezoar is fitted into their hip. There, I find a rounded tumescence the size of a hare's skull. It yields to pressure, although not far. Beneath, the pith feels like mouse bones chewed and compacted, baby teeth compressed into a calcium gnarl.

"I was their first or near enough to their first, at least. They found me almost a century ago, half buried in the corpses of a town whose name I have now forgotten, nearly dead myself. I remember blinking at the smoke-scrimmed sky. I remember the flies on my lips. It was warm and the sky was blue, and their army—" The plague doctor flinches away, malachite gaze hollow, haunted. Their hands shut into fists. "I suppose I would have died if they had not taken me. If they had not used me as their experiment. Their lord—our countries were at war, theirs and mine. They told me later there were orders to ensure there wouldn't be survivors. So. I was lucky. I suppose."

A snap of laughter, like a spine crisply bisected.

"They gave me a choice. They told me that I could come with them. I-in retrospect, I suppose it wasn't a choice at all. What child agrees to die? I said yes and they claimed me as theirs."

I can hear the village murmuring to itself, a drowsing soliloquy, like an old drunk repeating the name of the stars. Somewhere behind us, a hawk screams, a thing dies choking, and there's the soft sound of wingbeats lofting a meal to the nest.

"I became a—a test environment for them. Every new idea, every concoction, every configuration of viscera, they would measure its effectiveness against my body's responses. Together, we learned how much belladonna a small child might stomach, how a pig's heart may adequately substitute for its human counterpart, how tumors may grow from week to week. Slowly, there was less and less of me, and one day—"

They palm the seat of the bezoar, almost affectionate.

"Eventually, *this* was all that remained. A membranous sac of cells and nerves, a sampling of brain, enough raw material with which to grow new organs, new limbs. I wonder sometimes if this consciousness is the same, if I am the same, or if I am a mere fabrication, strung together by circumstances."

"There is nothing wrong with being a monster."

Their mouth bends. "You always know the right things to say."

Questions circle: how come, why. An entire history to vivisect and catalogue, weigh in the cup of a story, every anecdote no doubt more fascinating than the last. And then a thought: is this what humanity feels like? *Selfish?* These experiences are not mine to flense and frame, not mine to own, reuse in future conversations. Yet, I crave the answers, regardless.

"Were there others like you?"

"No. Not then. I was the only one. It makes sense that they've diversified since. Insurance against another runaway. More importantly, if their objective is to standardize a cure of mortality, it would make sense to use as many—"

A breath, a pause, and I can almost see the eddies of fate arrange themselves around us, fortune and history settling like a powdering of ice. I could walk away. I should, I should. I still could. "I don't care."

"I understand."

"But *you* do. Which, unfortunately, makes all the difference." I smile, slightly jagged. "Shall we return to the village? We've things to do."

~

"Your eyes were green before." And they'd tasted of lime and sweat and ice, had dissolved on my tongue like crème. I had eaten those like I'd eaten the heart, the hand.

"I'm certain," says the surgeon, fingers threading together. His new eyes are silver, like starlight strained and sieved, stainless save for the pinholes of his pupils. "That you believed they were green. Green is a very beautiful color."

No longer do the surgeons speak in echoes, the madrigal of their voices finally split. For their evening meal, they wear no masks, only skin and burlap robes, and they laugh like they're proletariat-raised, full of brashness. The children *adore* them. The youngest attach to their knees, their arms, tugging them every which way. The older children weaponize stories: accounts of their fastidiousness; descriptions of a fox they'd sighted in the woods, its tail a tongue of blood; philosophies newly improvised from the wisdom they'd culled from the guts of a stag. Anything that might elicit attention; a glance, the curve of a smile, or best of all: a word of approval, more precious than any opal.

The normalcy rankles. It reeks of rehearsal. I glance to where my plague doctor sits, spine straight, hands clasped over the table. Their plate is laden with cheeses, frost-bleached grapes, cold cuts thick-rind with fat. Nothing has been touched. As I watch, my plague doctor leans into conversation with the deep-voiced surgeon; their jaw clenching, unclenching, juddering with the effort of restraint.

"What *are* you?"

I look back to the surgeon-saint to my right. He smiles, only lips, no teeth. He and his cohorts had seemed indifferent to me in the cold morning—the third jabbers with the children, agreeable as a grandfather—but it might have been there were other things to distract them then: the stilted theatre that is every first meeting, the pleasures of such ceremony, the cipher of my plague doctor's distaste. "You're clearly not human. An aquatic creature, perhaps? Not a rusalka, no. I know the rusalka intimately. Your eyes—" He raises his hand, fingers splayed. Moves closer, closer, until his nails scratch my lips. *"Fascinating."*

I smile, *all* teeth. "I'm told."

The surgeon retracts, fingers balling, even as he lays his

hand atop the table. Behind him, two girls—one wide-set, with chestnut hair too thick to bind, the other slim as a needle—maneuver a cauldron to the table. Their stew is redolent of carrots, yams, parsnips, all slightly old; onions cooked till the sweetness bled from them; beef and marrow and boiled-down bones. "That was presumptuous of me."

"Yes."

"What can I ask you, then? Could we talk about the weighting of the stars above the night-bruised seas, and what happens when one falls into the abyss? Or whether pelicans converse in French when outside of human view? I'd love—" Shoulders slant forward. His expression becomes one of languorous interest, conspiratorial. "—to know what it is like in the deeps. What do you do? How do you interact with one another? Do you have a civilization? Are you feral?"

I allow myself, for the gash of a moment, to remember what I once possessed: the abyssal ocean, the song in those depths like swimming down the black throat of a god; the searing colors moting my sisters' coils, sapphire and quartz crushed into constellations, patterns and prisms of incandescence spiraling through the dark, our tails in endless, restless motion; our mother's eyes colossal, phosphorescent; our father's ribs, still studded with our egg sacs, his heartbeat in our veins. I'd been happy there. I could have been happy there forever.

"I'll tell you." I look up at the sky, a faultless blue, cold as the heart of a king. "But only as payment in a fair exchange, only if you agree to a game."

"And what game is that?" Oh, that hunger in his gaze, sharp as salt.

"Twice more." I raise two fingers. "I'd see you repeat your miracles; scoop out those grey eyes, return to us in the morning with a gaze of amber, emerald, cobalt—whatever you'd like to pretend it has always been."

Like a child caught with his fingers spooled around the heart of another boy, he smiles; slyness, not shyness communicated in the lidding of his gaze, his eyes unrepentant beneath long, curling lashes. He jerks his head. "And if we allow you to bear witness twice again, what do you promise us in sacrifice?"

His voice wreathes itself with the lilt of ritual.

"My heart. My past. The six hundred names of the hadal mothers, the bibles of the squids, the colors that you can only see when you are there in the nothing, there in the deep. Anything you ask or require."

"Anything at all?"

I look again to where my plague doctor sits, their own dialogue concluded.

"Yes."

❦

So, they do it again, with us and the children in attendance.

The first surgeon undoes the lock of his wrist and removes his hand without ceremony, no blood or untidy bouquet of nerves, bones glistening white. A single rotation, assisted by the downward swing of a cleaver.

The second surgeon extracts his eyes with equal uneventfulness: a delicate application of forceps, no more than that. Only at the end does he assert strength. A sharp tug; the optic nerves detach, a splattering trail of moist hues.

And the third, he makes no use of tools. Instead, he pares his shoulder of fabric, baring his chest and its puckered brown nipple, before peeling back cutis and muscle with his nails. Beneath, the ribs are revealed to be grotesquely architectured, the striations of calcium shored up by stucco, so to accommodate the hole hacked into their midst. Inside the man-made cavity, epauletted by amethyst and mica, his heart shudders, as though horrified by the presence of an audience.

He removes the organ without any overtures of agony, and the village howls like dogs in celebration.

～

"Are you certain you know what you're doing?" My plague doctor's breath blooms white in the dark of the shed.

"Not entirely. But I think—" I smack my lips. The night is frost and sheets of falling snow, like flecks of crystal through which the moon is refracted a thousand times over. It is so quiet without the children and their baying, all of them asleep. I wonder what we would do should one of them discover us here. "I think what we must do is displace their godhood, remind their devotees that these are just men who bleed."

My plague doctor sighs in counterpoint, expression morose, but they do not hesitate to retrieve what I'd requested: the heart, the hands, the staring eyes . . . "There are simpler ways."

"My husband was a foolish man. But he understood one

thing well." I move the new oblations in place, thumb stroking across still-warm ventricles. "For the falling star and the rising ape to meet, the former must first be debased. No myth can remain terrifying when you've seen it broken and beaten, rendered as toothless as an old crone."

No reply save for a subtle retexturing of their breath, the gap between inhalations infinitesimally smaller, the length of their exhalations protracted. Then: fingers gently clasp my shoulder. No words are needed. I smile into the gloom and my teeth glimmer like knives.

And I eat as my plague doctor unravels the lynx's corpse, removes the souvenirs we intend to leave in our wake.

Hand, heart, unblinking eyes—

I savor them all.

The hand, this time, is flavored with copper, its cartilage fractures like glass; the heart is a mouthful of brine and fermented raspberry; the eyes burst into effervescence, peculiarly tasteless. Beneath every note, however, I find Samson, the stink and salt of him, his fear intaglioed into a bloodied aftertaste. If I focus, I can almost hear the syncopation of his pulse: pained and urgent.

He did not die easy. He did not die quick either. His flesh is pungent with trauma, acidic, nearly mush, textured like rotted shrimp. I swallow every bite, nonetheless. Waste is deplorable, no matter how pitiful or poorly seasoned the victuals.

III

The Third Night

We wake to a commotion.

I uncoil from the bed and tweak aside a curtain flap, look out into the village: one of the surgeons is on his knees, hunched over, like a penitent in the throes of flagellation. Someone'd bound his eyes with a strip of bloodied cloth. He moans. He claws furrows into his cheeks. Around me, a noose of staring children echo his agony.

"I think they noticed." I turn to my companion.

"So fortunate that they are gods then and not men." My plague doctor sits up, their hair a cloud of knots, voice husked. "Kings would have us swinging from the gallows by now."

Their tone is mild despite their words, allayed further by a misalignment of their mouth, a not-quite smile that could have been, in a different light, a grimace instead. I twitch a shoulder upwards. "Perhaps."

"Perhaps," they echo, sloughing their cotton robes as they

do. In their motions, there is neither seduction nor pretense of decorum, merely efficiency. While they dress, I study the mathematics of scars inlaid into their spine, their shoulders, the sloping of their pelvis. "I suppose it is time for the second act."

Appearance is everything.

Remember this when you've forgotten all else.

"I did not know that saints could weep." The malice is starkly unsubtle, its stridence so anomalous that I blink at its manifestation.

The surgeon labors to his feet, one knee and then the next; breath whining between his teeth. Blood has dried into black tributaries, sectioning his features like a butcher's chart. His grimace is blotched with ochre. "I see, I see, I *see*. What a blessing these eyes are. Never have I beheld the truth more clearly."

"And what is *that* truth?"

"Even a mutt may gaze upon a god if it is sly enough to wait until the divine sleeps." The surgeon staggers, loses traction. He slips. A *crunching* noise: an applause of cartilage and ligament, tearing, snapping beneath the descent of the body's weight. But the surgeon does not scream; he spits, fresh blood and green-yellow phlegm, bits of bone like half-digested baby teeth.

My plague doctor grins beneath their mask. The expression is pure savagery. They stalk forward, and I follow in silhouette, my profile muddled by stratas of warm fur. A stratagem that my companion does not explain, only implements after obtaining consent. I pluck at the collar, tense beneath its captured heat.

"I will keep those words in mind for when and if I meet a god." The sound of my plague doctor's voice is poison. They crouch before the surgeon, head cocked, the drape of their robes like a framework of wings. "Let me know if you meet one. I'd love to see if my manners might please them."

"Mongrel *dog*—"

"If only words weren't meaningless." An upward stroke of steel; the surgeon's head ricochets back. Blood gouts, blistering heat. My plague doctor carves him open from philtrum to forehead, butterflies the flesh so it weeps into flaps.

Fabric ripples onto the snow, the paleness debauched by gore. The children mill in place, uncertain noises pulsing in their throats like drumbeats.

"Your saints promised you perfection." No smugness in the pronouncement. No discernible emotion at all. My plague doctor clutches their knife loosely, reverse-grip, its edge now ribbed with vermillion. "But how can they give you that when they themselves are so fallible? So mortal? Everything they've shown you was just . . . *lies*. Trickery. Sleights of hand."

With each word, however, their enunciation becomes more staccato. Each syllable is a detonation. "Look at him and tell me if this wretch deserves worship."

The surgeon bears animal eyes in his sockets. Lynx eyes, I wager, from the shine and the shape of the iris. They are held in place by a web of pink tissue, keloided, beaded with warm pus and dandelion blooms of fresh nerves.

The result of the mischief we wrought in the shed is hideous.

"Ungrateful—" His voice has taken on a stridulatory resonance, an unpleasant buzzing, like a cicada taught to speak. The surgeon staggers upright, one eye making orbits in its hollow. Momentum disgorges the other. It thumps against his cheek, the optic nerve overgrown with extraneous tissue. Eyelids flutter loosely, devoid of corneal support, concaving into the hollow.

"Look at him," my plague doctor repeats. This time, they do not resist the impulse to sneer.

A scream cuts through the tableau before we learn of the children's assessment, whether they find the debasement of their saint repugnant or revelatory. As one, they stampede to the loci of the wailing: one of the smaller cottages, a slant of tiling and wood clinging parasitically to its neighbour's foundation.

We follow, my plague doctor and I, pulled forward by the noise. It is not dissimilar from the sound that Luke made as the surgeons threaded his soul into his carcass: raw-throated, expunged without consideration for air or damage to the esophagus.

The door is slammed open. The children barge in. I join the mass of bodies, craning a look around their shoulders. The antumbra reveals little: broad shapes, crates, shelves stacked close as vertebrae. Movement that segues into snuffling, chewing. A shuffle of footsteps. Crying. Someone invokes a pantheon of names; someone gasps; someone retching onto the flooring. The air, already stinking of musk and mildew, grows acid.

A pane of morning sunlight fractures across the dark, divulging the scene at last. The surgeon with the voice of bass stoops over a body, his mouth wedged in the solar plexus. It is the girl whose abode we'd taken. She lays under the surgeon, whimpering ceaselessly, arms above her head. Still alive, in spite of her disembowelment, and agonizingly so.

The surgeon wraps fingers around exposed ribs, tugs hard. The calcium scaffolding comes apart like slabs of meringue. He plants the heel of his palm against the breastbone and pushes, freeing more space for his chin. The surgeon uses the jut of it like a shovel, nuzzles upwards before he plunges headfirst into the spooled offal, begins to feast again. He savors each gulp, moans into the motion.

"You were right."

Luke.

"You were right about the saints." His voice is high and aching, terrified. I hadn't realized that he'd been part of the watching mass, had been unable to differentiate him from the columns of starved limbs, and the intent faces. "They're monsters. They're murderers. We—"

"Shut up, Luke."

One of the other boys, older, more muscular, with a thatching of dark hair outlining his jowls; he plucks a spade from the wall, hefts the tool into his grip. Luke gawks at him, fishmouthing, voice serrated from hysteria. He raises open palms, expression beseeching: a priest at the death of time, evangelizing for a heaven long crumbled into nostalgia.

"No! Why can't you see? I—"

The older boy bounces the handle against his palm, and brings the blade down on Luke's skull with a crack. The moment before impact, I turn and lunge towards my plague doctor.

It is too late.

A weight connects with my temple, sharp. Hard enough that my vision erupts into polyps, ultraviolet starbursts spidering across the world until everything is snow. Darkness comes shortly after and I go down, my last sight that of the plague doctor, knives in hand, surrounded by hunched shadows that look almost like wolves.

~

The pain is less than I thought it'd be.

Duller. Vaguer, distributed across the longitude of my abdomen. Blinking to sluggish awareness, I'd anticipated the memory of the fisherman's knife, a tactile delirium inherited from past incarnations. Incisions made along the spine. The skin, drying to salt-crust, being peeled back after it's first been loosened by a blade. The air blistering on bare muscle. An experience like drowning.

But no, this is different.

I take my time in indexing the myriad sensations. The delicate tenterhook-tugging laddered down my ribs, perceptible only when I breathe. Pinpricks of sharpness, timed to my heartbeat. The tectonic motions in my abdominal cavity, subtle, precise, like continents resettling.

Then: a cut.

My eyelids flare open. I judder upwards, a dying fish, scis-

soring from the table on which I've been placed, animal biol-
ogy conspiring against my efforts in counterfeiting oblivion. I
don't—*can't*—scream; my throat refuses the exercise. But the
body, so treacherously human, endeavors to do so, anyway.
Copper blooms wetly in my lungs. I choke.

"You're awake." The voice is amused: a cold, lithe baritone
that could deepen into a bass with some effort.

I drag my tongue over chapped lips, tasting their glaze of
dried blood, bile. The darkness is cool, unexpectedly humid, for
all that it is flame-limned, an orange afterlight contouring the
rafters above me. Dried spices pendulate above me: purple basil,
saffron, strings of allspice slotted together like rosaries.

"I am," I croak. "Some measure of awake, yes."

"Give me a moment in that case. The anesthesia should
be wearing out any time now." Something slices between the
tendons of my left wrist, glides upwards towards the elbow, saws
deeper. My arm unlaces into agony. I hiss.

"You're remarkably resilient."

He laughs. I do not. Instead, I crane a look downwards along
my chest and grimace at the view. I've been meticulously vivi-
sected. Every one of my organs has been removed and relocated
into glass containers, steeped in a pale preservative the color of
gold. No move has been made to sever them from the vascular
system, however. Everything remains interconnected, joined
either by function or blood vessels. The result is strangely pleas-
ing to the eye: a crosshatching of arteries and alimentary ca-
nals, an intricate map.

"Does it hurt?"

I shudder as he separates my left arm into two halves before sectioning them into dermis, fat, and muscle. He then migrates a palmful of adipose tissue onto a small ornate scale, the wet lump excreting translucent oils.

"Yes."

But not as much, I suspect, as he wishes.

The lynx-eyed surgeon laughs again, the firelight turning his eyes indigo. "You really are remarkable. Most would have died of shock."

I don't answer. I count each inhalation instead and memorize the strangeness of the act, every repetition compounding nuance, bringing to attention something new and unpleasant. The surgeon has begun humming to himself, a jaunty tune I recognize from evenings with the ambitious bourgeois. It is, hypocritically, a song about inuring the weak, of the hare hunting the fox.

"What *are* you?" he breathes, voice husked like a lover's.

"My husband's court told me I was a mermaid."

Mermaid. A word that demonstrates the ineptitude of human language, and the species' predisposition for infantilizing the unknown. I have seen the woodcuts, the illustrations, the portraits of bare-breasted women with voluptuous tails, both equally ill-suited for the deep water. But palatability is prized over accuracy. It is easier to market a nymph than a viperfish.

"Is that so? Well, the paintings do your kind no justice." His tone maintains its conversational timbre even as he debones my forearm; ulna and radius extracted, laid out on white gauze. "I have to admit. I am surprised. You lack swim bladders? I'd have thought—"

"In the roof of my mouth."

The words drag him forward.

"In the seat of my skull. Beneath the firmament of the brain."

"You're lying to me," the lynx-eyed surgeon says. But I can tell that he is curious. His fingers wend around the handle of a bone saw, palm clenching along its spine. "Although I'm not certain what for."

I say nothing. I wait.

He circles around behind me, hands and arms expediently armored in dense leather gloves, an intelligent precaution. A clatter of metal. The bone saw is set down. His fingers cup my chin, thumbs boring into the hollows above the lower mandibles. "Why? Why are you lying to me? There is no advantage to be found in falsehood. You must under—"

Man mistakes his own experiences as the canvas on which all truths are drawn. He is rarely correct in this respect. Once disemboweled, flayed, pinioned to the table like an exotic specimen, a human becomes tractable. But I am not human, have never been human, shall never *be* human. Not for all the bodies a prince might place on an altar to a dying witch.

I rear upwards, mouth distending. My teeth close on the hinge of the surgeon's jaw and bend. They perforate the underside of his mouth, impale his tongue. He gurgles a screeching objection and pinwheels backwards, hands slapping at the air. I follow, dragged by his momentum; sinew gashed to rags, skin torn, viscera slopping free of their containment. Something in me pulls taut. Something *snaps*.

We fall together, the surgeon and I, tangled body parts and shattering glass. I drive fingers deep into the soft of his obliques. His flesh gives and I pull myself up one gobbet of muscle at a time, until I find bone to grip. He screams again. I don't let him stop.

His jaw, I devour: molar and membrane chewed to a paste, swallowed. Before he can move, I plunge my head down again, this time into the hollow of his throat. I crunch through clavicle, barely pausing to taste, tongue snaking into the pulmonary tract. I gorge myself on his pain. I eat him alive.

After everything that he has done, this seems like fair restitution.

~

I leave nothing.

I suckle my knuckles clean of spinal fluids, gouge the offal from under my nails. The flavor is uniform, bizarre: a medicinal sweetness like something artificial, granular in texture. I palm the slick floor for anything I might have missed, and find the ridge of a hip bone to absently chaw as I weigh my options.

It is late. Twelve hours must have passed, at least. The sky through the gap in the roof is black. Moonlight pours through the incision, a haze of cold silver. To my surprise, no one has come to investigate the wailing, not even at its inchoate apex. Perhaps they'd grown accustomed to such tormented noise, have learned to edit its cadences from their daily routines, to disregard what cannot be remedied.

Perhaps they enjoy it.

I lean back against the leg of a table, hair matted over my face and bare flesh. Likewise, the room is webbed with desiccated viscera, liver and stomach and gallbladder all withered to scabrous clumps. Inside the casement of my torso, new organs have fruited. My skin, laced with the ink-spill of a discarded venous system, is similarly rejuvenated: no wounds, no gnarled cicatrice, nothing to memorialize what has transpired. Only a faintly nacreous smoothness, as though of opal coaxed to reluctant life. My initial supposition was correct: the surgeons' flesh is uncommonly restorative, better than a slug of ambrosia, or any cut from the body of the butchered divine, hidden away by the Abbess of Wasps so she can hoard its gift of eternal life.

Carefully, I pluck a shriveled vein from my skin and rub it between my fingers until it disintegrates, until it is black chalk dust billowing from a cupped palm. I swallow bone-meal, swallow marrow, allow the taste to dissipate, before at last I let myself be afraid.

It is a strange feeling to hold, my courage sieving between my fingers. I was not afraid when my prince dragged me from the ocean, or when he made my sisters into trophies, their bones shucked and swapped for steel rods, their arteries flushed with formaldehyde. But I am frightened now, and the absence of my plague doctor is a mouth in the nadir in my belly, eating its way through the womb's wolf-light up to the uncaring sky.

A howling rives through the quiet, seven voices to an octave, orgasmic.

I suck the chill from between clenched teeth. Exhale. For the first time, my breath frosts in the air. An omen, perhaps, but one that I have neither time nor tool to decode. I sway to my feet, the surgeon's garments taken for my own, and pad towards the door. Outside, the taiga waits for me, the bodies of the spruce like teeth in a corpse's smile.

❧

A drag of vermillion across the trampled snow. Bloodied palm-prints clawed into the white. Countless footprints, but only one set suggests that its owner might have staggered, might have fallen, weighted down by their robes, before they wrestled equilibrium from the cold and shambled onwards, blades between their knuckles and wolves at their heels. No bile or piss, however, no pus or reek of infection. No vomit. Only red blood blackening to ice. They bled my plague doctor, but not with the intention to kill.

To hobble, yes. To slow, to ensure against the risk of a fair game. When some children play at slaughtering, the pig must always die, or else what point is there in pursuing the squealing hog through the woods and the wild?

Between the trees, smears of light crisscross the dark, like the marks a hand might scratch onto a wall. I follow the footprints into the wilderness, pausing occasionally to stoop and break loose chunks of burgundy ice, suckling on the crystalline fragments until they melt. I can taste my plague doctor, their waning heartbeat.

Someone screams, sharp as a crack of bone.

And as though summoned by the noise, the wind comes again, almost tangible, so cold that it burns blue through the pores and under the skin, cauterizing all notion of sensation. But that first ragged gust is deceptive, scarcely more than an overture, a clearing of the throat. With its second exhalation, the wind brings a storm, a rippling diamantine Ragnarök, strangling the taiga in salt.

Hoarfrost limns my lashes and my lips. My fingers blister in their stolen gloves. I sink into the snow. It piles higher as I walk, ankle-length first, then rising to the height of my thighs. Still, I plow on, deeper, deeper into the pale woods, the plague doctor's agony held against the roof of my mouth, like a compass made of copper and heat.

The world flattens into a painting: light and dark and nothing in between, no depth and barely any color. Even the torches seem blanched of hue, their luminance dulled to something spectral. It reminds me of the deepwater. I pull my collar over my mouth, pant into the fabric, keep moving, following the map that they'd left me. It is an atlas of ruin, charted with the corpses of the young villagers, throats and bellies gutted, the snow like so much salt in the bowl of their gaping mouths.

The cold, I discover, has a way of eliding all of the mind's excess, its propensity for fussing over unimportant details. Like that itching behind the huddle of your collar, the certainty of surveillance. The fatigue, heavy and sleepy, curled into your joints. The rough scrape of the air in your lungs. Fear, like a second heart beating itself to death against your temples, like love, like something not unlike love.

Such petty concerns do not survive the cold. In a blizzard as tempestuous as this, there is only space for simplicity: the compulsion to put one foot after another, to draw one breath after the next.

I pass a boy impaled to a tree, like some messiah left for the crows, skewered through the palms and windpipe, the hatchet's handle tipping his chin back. Blood clusters between his clavicles like frosted garnets. He cannot have been dead for long, yet nothing mammalian remains in his mien, his fingers black and stiff beneath the grey-green rime.

Impulsively, I kiss the poor corpse on its frozen cheek. For luck or spite, I can no longer tell. His lantern lies on its side, glass cracked and weeping oil. Briefly, I consider taking it for my own, salvaging what heat it can still produce. But the fire, delicious as it would be on skin gone cold and numb, will forfeit my position. We are playing a game, they and I and my plague doctor, ancient as the practice of wanting, and I will not lose.

Somewhere, someone begins to sing. It would be twin to the dirge that marched us to the village except for how it's been gored of vowels, is only consonants now, like so much cartilage, gristle, and mumble. From the west, six paces ahead, cascades a counterpoint, like a cupful of crushed glass. From the east, the south, more voices: an entire vocabulary of predator noises braided into conversation.

I stop and strain to make sense of their singing, as though the act of stillness might wring meaning from those syllables. They are wolves in this freezing void, more than wolves, more than human, less than both, the ebb and gibber of their voices the only sound in the wind. They signal to one another with barks, sharp yelps. My lungs fill with ice as I wait, wait and listen, wait and watch for a sign. There is a fifth voice, a sixth, a seventh, wrapping together in shining waves, before the ninth slits the air with its shrieking hunger, and all of us blur into motion.

The children, the butchers, the saints' little trove of youthful organs, those wolf-whelps, are quick, but I am faster, a blade brought to the throb of a vein. I am a mother of monsters, better than any of my young. I race their fires, footsteps falling in the slats between their screams, every one of us moving northwards, steering by that cry which seems to say *Come, come and bear witness to the slaughter.*

Halfway, a girl explodes from the taiga, lips peeled back from yellow incisors, her hair a storm. Black tendrils whorl and writhe along the thin white blades of her shoulders, crawl into her grimace. Her mouth is bruise-blue, bruise-dark. She cocks her head and measures me with chatoyant eyes, incurious. Her pink tongue laps at the air.

We lunge together, two actors in a story so old that its rhythms are recorded in marrow, retold with every new birth, repeated with every fresh death. Her spear—a jag of glass lashed to a thin branch—shreds my earlobe as it passes. I turn, cinch her arm in my teeth, bite down so deeply I can wrap my lips around bone, jerk my head upwards. Her flesh unravels, rolls up like a tattered sleeve. Blood gouts, freezing to rubies before it can find the ground.

The girl inhales to screech, one hitching breath. I bury its denouement in the cellar of my throat, mouth locking over her windpipe, her spine. Her vertebrae break with the crisp, dewed noise of an apple's skin when it is first pierced. She crumples, I follow her down, palm molded to her skull, taking only as much as I need, just a thimble of cider-sweet meat. Her eyes are still open when I lift my head and knuckle her blood from my lips, a rind of frost already beginning to crust on pale irises; the shive-light transmutes the ice into a dowry of diamonds.

Her blood beats hot in the rooms of my heart. In the after-taste, the sum of her denudes itself: past, present, and devoured potential, preserved at their brightest, their most spectacu-lar. Every way she could have been more, more than a feral half-thing—I think I remember her from the village, but that felt like a life ago—skulking through the woods, more than appetite, more than a clot of red rusting on my tongue.

I blink ghosts—a thousand flickering instances of the girl, darting between the tree line—from my vision. I wonder if these hallucinations had plagued the surgeons too, if the taking of an organ is indistinguishable from its consumption, and if so, did the surgeons suffer or did they employ these delusions as somme-liers, curating a menu of experiences, each scintilla of sensation arranged to magnify the next? The powerful have always made meals of the small. I lick a film of gore from my teeth. The bliz-zard moans.

"Sorry," I tell the blackness, uncertain, feeling as though that at least is owed of me. The taiga says nothing. The ghosts say less. And the cold keeps tunneling into my bones, calcium shivering to crystal.

More baying, long and low. The firelight converges to a sin-gle shuddering point. As the children scream their triumph, I follow their wailing voices down, down into that dark.

~

I find my plague doctor with their back to a broken oak, spine rested against its stump, head lolled onto their collarbone. The snow is vermillion beneath them, the color fresh. A dead boy lies across their lap, arms crossed over his chest, and the sight of them is almost bucolic, a summer idyll with its colors inverted: wheat golds and blue sky exchanged for venous red and white.

"They managed to surprise me." My plague doctor sighs. They stroke fingers through the corpse's hair, their mask gone, their eyes green as summer, a pinpoint of inhuman fluorescence radiating from the door of each pupil. "I am tired now. I think I'm done running. Seventeen dead. Will you remember this number for me when I am gone? I think I impressed myself a little."

"Remember it yourself—"

"I'm dying." They smile when they tell me this, relieved. My plague doctor moves their arm and their wounds are revealed, entrails disgorging in cold, grey loops. Their blood had frozen to an alphabet and it is a love letter spilled over the corpse they hold, it is a living will, it is instruction. But I ignore them. I'm not ready. Not yet, not yet. "Slowly, and without particular hope for recovery."

I don't lie to them nor do I portend inevitabilities, and instead cup the drooping viscera in my palm. Tenderly, with a girl's reverence, as though the coils were expensive ribbons that I might thread through my hair. What surprises us both is the cry that escapes, the tiniest of whining gasps, and my plague doctor's eyes becomes effulgent. Something like love flits between us.

I press my head to the chapel of their chest, that nameless corpse displaced. Carefully, I fit myself into their arms, body curled into a question, their intestines in the bowl of my hands, and I hold them there, hold us there, my breathing metered by the diminuendo of their pulse. Slower, slower, until each inhalation is elevated to an event, unique in its infrequency.

"We had a good run." They laugh at the phrasing. Blood spasms between my fingers, scalding. It couldn't have been more than an hour, surely, but already I've forgotten what it is like to be warm, what it is like to be anything but numb.

"Don't speak."

"It doesn't matter," the plague doctor ripostes, their languor infuriating. For a wild moment, I'm subsumed by hypotheticals: what if I were to devour them? Bone and brain and bezoar, the last swallowed whole and unbroken. Would their cells, once edited into nutrients, then parasitize mine? Colonize and civilize the crenellations of my brain, develop into a ghost, a disparate consciousness. If I could answer this with any certainty, I'd consume them in a heartbeat, preserve them in every chapter of my body. I'd do anything but watch them die. Even if payment for their longevity isn't shared tenancy of this body, but complete monopoly. Better I be reduced to miscreant daydreams of the ocean than be alive without them. Whatever it takes. Anything. Anything, so long as they stay with me. "There's no point."

"The bezoar—"

"Too much damage." Their kindness is traumatic to endure. "It is alright. There are worse ways to die. I promise. I've seen them, lived them. I—"

The exposition is interrupted by labored coughing. I look up. My plague doctor bleeds from every cavity: ears, mouth, nostrils, tear ducts. Estuaries of wine that taste on my tongue of the taiga and the sea, salt and soil grown rich on the dead. Of trout excessively seasoned, of my palm on the plague doctor's cheek, of futures foreshortened, of a kiss that never was, and all at once, I am drowning in loss, and I need them to stay, no matter the price. I'd slice my larynx clean, make soup of the ribbons. I'd peel every word from my vocabulary. Anything, everything, so long as I can keep them anchored to this life.

"Please don't talk," I whisper, my impotence a knife through my gut. So many years spent an exile from my own voice, and this is all I can muster: platitudes, weakly murmured into cold and turgid flesh. "Please don't talk. Please don't talk. Please don't talk. Please don't. Don't—don't die."

The entreaty is an embarrassment. I cringe at its infantile architectonics, at how maudlin it all sounds, but my plague doctor only chuckles, their fingers wefted into my hair. A thumb finds the parabola of my lower lip, nail stroking against needle-teeth. "You should go."

"No."

"There's no point in dying here."

"There's no point in being alive either," I counter, vicious, relentless. "Where am I to go? If you die, I can't—"

My plague doctor does not hear me. I don't think they can. Their caress becomes rhythmic, restless, broad strokes that chart the road between cheek and chin. "That wasn't the case when we first decided to travel. I remember precisely how you looked. Standing in the square in your ragged finery, radiant in your newfound freedom. You looked"—another paroxysm, another dribble of claret—"like you'd seen the world unroll like a map and there were no borders, no boundaries, nowhere you couldn't go. You were *so* beautiful."

They kiss me then. Through the hair matted to my brow, their mouth wet with warmth. They kiss me and my heart seizes with grief. "Bury me, my love, and take a lock of my hair with you. Carry me through the centuries. I think I'd like to share, just a little, in what immortality is like."

I begin to keen.

"You don't have to. I can be a romantic fool."

"It's not that. It's not. It's—"

"It is alright." They sigh. "This is not my first death."

And that sigh becomes the sound of muscles slackening beneath skin and sinew, of a body unmaking itself from the rote and routine of living, one stitch at every stage of exhale, liver and lungs and lymph slumping into obsoletion. I clutch at my plague doctor, palsied by my weeping, and I am deserted by every thought save these:

That I want to die here, mired in the cold. That I want to race them to Death's carriage, exceeding their pace but only just, never going so far as to be unable to turn and corset their fingers in mine. That eternity is a worthless bauble without their conversation. That I would follow them into the demise of the universe where every heaven and each hell is shuttered, and there is nothing of us but motings of wan light, and there is no bodily apparatus with which to express affection, no recourse save to glow weakly in worship until at last, such things are swallowed too by the dark.

That I would love them even then.

As long as a moiety of conscious thought persists, I will love them.

I will love them to the death of days.

Succumbed to fatalism, I do not stir when a hand clinches my shoulder and another, papered in leather, explores the anachronism of teeth and temple, my thalassic nature more apparent now. A thumb caresses the gills fronding my jaws; frosted over, they crack painlessly where pressure is gratuitously applied. I do not pay attention to any of these things, though, not until knuckles impact my face, hard enough that the nasal bone fenestrates. Thin slivers of calcium and cartilage embed beneath my orbital sockets, spackle the adjacent skin. One works through the curtain of flesh that is my cheek. Another spears an eyeball.

The second blow comes before I can orient: a slap this time, imperious.

"Wake up, little fish."

"Wake."

"Wake."

I stare into the blizzard through a rinse of scarlet.

Silhouettes in the writhing snow, ominously spectral: the children, like a jury of deaths, standing witness to my sentencing. In the foreground, in sharper focus, the triptych of charnel saints, those dread surgeons, gazing solemnly down upon my prone frame. They are without masks or perceivable injury, features rendered handsome anew. I think I can see something of Luke's mordance in the spokes of their expressions, overlaid by Samson's ferality, his grin unutterably obscene through the window of those three's mouths.

"I should have made you scream longer." I laugh shakily. Each time I blink, the needle of bone works itself deeper, tearing at the corneal layer. Soon enough, my vision is halved, the ruin of that eye marked by a gout of warm fluids, trickling tear-like down my frozen cheek. "But you tasted foul and it would have taken too much time. Still, I regret it."

The one I had ingurgitated, stripped of sinew and sheets of muscle, whose ribs I had fractured so I could better worm into the abdominal cavity and undo the heart from where it latches to the diaphragm. Who I ate alive, vellicating organs with my nails, scraping tunica from the vulnerable entrail, while he twitched like a fish on the line: these chunks like condiments for bigger swathes of meat, and also a way to expedite his consumption. That one, he glares at me with leadlight eyes, teeth gritted.

"I won't make that mistake," he says.

A sudden fractious movement beneath me: the plague doctor, lurching into startled awareness.

"I told you to run." Agony in that hoarse verbalization, their hand fumbling for mine. "Why didn't you run?"

I slant a bleak smile at them. "You're here."

Their grip tightens.

"Idiot."

꩜

They leash us to two wizened birches, the trees dead long before this winter, ossified by some meteorological alchemy. I'd thought initially they would leave us staked there, let the cold take us. But the surgeons had different plans.

The children, skin bruised by exposure to the bitter weather, extremities hypothermic, fingertips black from the gelid condition of their blood, rush through the taiga, seeking what wood they can, any kindling they can salvage, no matter how esoteric its former nature. Our funerary pyre becomes a study in boreal archaeology: a drift of dead branches, ancient pine cones, desiccated moss, and corpses hacked loose from icy integuments. Fat burns gorgeously, after all, and with such succulent fragrance. My husband's kingdom taught me this.

"Tell me about your sisters," comes a ragged entreaty.

I jump at my plague doctor's voice, though not very far, not with my wrists bayoneted to the tree. I had thought them dead and been grateful for such. They had hung there for long minutes, slack, gore spewing from their belly, intestines like spoiled goldwork, its color bleached by the cold. In the tenebrous light, it is almost beautiful: the frost become diamantine paillettes, and I think of weddings. Not in vaulted halls where the air is insipid with sandalwood and spun sugar, a stink of powders. But in the taiga in spring, when the world has thawed, and there is green everywhere, green beneath my feet and green in the trees, wreathing the boughs like a bride's crown, green like the lambence of their eyes.

"Tell me about the deep. Tell me of your fathers, of your bathyal mothers. Tell me what it is like there in the dark water. Tell me if the stories are true. Do you sing men to their deaths? Do you drown maidens? Are the rusalka kin? Tell me," their voice falters. "Tell me your stories until the fire comes."

I do.

I tell them everything. I recite the chthonic scriptures,

the migratory cycles of the kelpies; my misgivings about how Scylla had been poorly represented, no more monster than Charybdis, who has become sweet in their dotage, too old to do more than faintly worry passing ships. I tell them of what happens when a sealwife renounces domesticity and decants herself into the water, how some husbands follow and why others do not, and what happens when a man gives himself wholly to the sea and its children. I recount each birth I've had, how we are haunted by our sisters. I tell them of the abyss, of the colors there, those hues mankind will never add to their tomes because they will never find their way to our homes, and we will drown them if they think to try.

"And your names?" asks my plague doctor, my beloved. "What power is there in your names that you can offer them while tongueless, mutilated by husbands?"

I try to answer, but suddenly, it's too late.

"So you know what we intend," says the surgeon with the bass voice. "You will both burn. Had you been less difficult, we might have made a harvest of you. We might have taken your skin and reaped your bones. We might have studied every inch of your sinew and vein. Paraded you through the museums, and placed you in the circuses of the world. They would have loved you. They would have known you. But now, you will be ash instead."

"Nothing but."

"*Ash.*"

The children begin to howl their praises.

"I read somewhere," says my plague doctor, "that there is

power to your kind's names, isn't there? Or was it in your voices? I can't remember. Not right now. But there was a reason your husband sliced out your tongue, was there not? He was afraid, one way or another, of the voice that beats in your lungs, your hurricane scream. You frightened him. How men fear things that can't be quieted."

Their laughter shears through the ice, through the crackle of the kindling as the embers burst and leap, and that rapacious inferno bulges beneath my plague doctor's feet. How carnivorous that sullen light, building in gusts, until not even the onslaught of snow might delay it. I watch as it clambers towards them, so eager to swallow them.

I begin to scream.

Yet my plague doctor remains insouciant, even smiling.

"You don't remember me, do you? The things that you did."

The surgeons stand silent for a time. Then:

"We don't remember meat."

"Meat."

"Meat."

At this, my plague doctor erupts again into lunatic laughter, louder this time, baying their mirth as though this tableau is as innocent as a drink in a warm tavern. Their viscera heaves, descends by another three inches, torn by the violence of their guffawing. I am mute again countenancing this horror, transfixed by a nihilistic certainty that this is better, that this is quicker, that them dying in this fashion is superior to an excruciating death by the fire.

"Well," says my plague doctor. "At least you won't forget her."

And they speak my name into the fire as the crash of their heart goes quiet and the loss is too much but the act somehow is enough, becomes fatwood for what follows.

What happens after feels as natural as falling, as grief, as flight: an effervescence which begins first as needlepoints of light within my breast before it becomes torrential, a devouring effulgence spreading as I imagine feathers might, downing my skin, the walls of my organs, my throat, the nadir of my being abruptly incandescent. I swallow a breath, exhale flame and it is not dissimilar from what seethes across my plague doctor's pyre, but it is cleaner, far cleaner: a celestial thing, bereft of fuel from unwilling flesh.

The surgeons retreat. The children shrink from what I have become.

But it is too late for all of us.

Once upon a time, a man wrote a parable about a mermaid who fell in love with a prince, and when she failed to kill him in his wedding bed, she evaporated to foam. I am melting, sluicing away to cinders and calcium first, to snarling bone. The body I'd held for long, that I'd held despite man's predations, that I'd held in captivity, held like a vow, a curse, a blasphemy, a wish for better things, combusts. I recall once there was an astronomer in my husband's court, who extolled the poetry of the universe, how numinous we were, despite the mucus and the blood we shed. *Stardust*, he'd said, inebriated with his own doctrine. We are made of *stardust*.

Or maybe, of primordial elements such as the ocean and the dark and the killing flame and love. Perhaps, my kind are conduits, our shape defined not by parentage but the things to which we'd yoked our beliefs. Perhaps, we are as any myths are: protean, impossible, exactly what we need to be.

Whatever the case, I burn them all for what they've done.

~

Morning comes, ashen through the gristle of the bare branches. I wake, aching, as its light sleets across my prone body, limbs coiled foetally atop a bed of charred figures, warped beyond identification. If anyone had survived last night's conflagration, I do not know as they are nowhere to be seen, and there are no tracks leading away from this place. Unseen, a songbird trills obeisances to the dawn, voice sweet, and I think immediately of my plague doctor, what they might say of its melody.

Except they are gone.

I look to where they had hung several feet away from me, the birch to which they were bound reduced to brushwork. Of my plague doctor, there is no trace. No. A lie, that. They are still here: a stubble of calcined fragments jutting from the cinders: teeth, a curve of bare skull, their mask, improbably intact. I can see their remains, limned by the dawn-light. Emboldened, I stagger to where they'd burned to nothing, crumbling onto my knees, hope banging a wild refrain through my pulse. I sift through the ash, still warm from the blaze. I search until I find it:

Their bezoar.

It is whole, without wound or seeming blemish: a glistening bolus the pigment and complexion of fresh liver, florid from whatever cardiac activity drives blood through its thin arteries.

I stroke a finger over the organ, and it frissons under the contact.

"You're safe," I tell the remnants of the slaughter, the indifferent taiga.

I do not yet know what to do with the organ, if metempsychosis is plausible, what with my dearth of medical knowledge, particularly in the vein of reconstruction. But my kind do not die until we are killed or until we relent to be consumed.

I have forever.

I will make this right again.

IV

Epilogue

It is done.

I place the bezoar into its aureate habitat, a wire-frame sphere with a gilded door, its insides cushioned with velvet and altricial down and sigils I'd labored for ten years to write, stooped over a magnifying glass thieved from a crypt, pricking my finger each time the ink thinks to clot. I gave them muscles stitched from the fibers of my gut, intestinal membrane first dried then bathed in chromium salts, so that their chimera body won't think to digest them. In this light, they seem beautiful, exposed as they are to the air. I will gown them with skin when we are ready. I will ask if they covet dermis or diamonds, some nacreous interstitiality. Whatever they want, I will place it at their feet.

Even their death.

My plague doctor draws a rattling breath, rouses in acts: each inhalation staccato, performed like a clockwork ballet. I pin my breath to the roof of my mouth. The tics and the spasms ease. For ballast, I made them bones of black onyx through which I'd laced steel; I needed them porous for the marrow.

"What—"

Copper fingers dart to a throat bridged by sutures, like the markings on the medical apparatus spread around us. The basement is dust and the debris of decades of research, the totality of human knowledge cannibalized for this single ambition. I'd autopsied practices, sacrosanct and putrid. I'd hunted the saints of medicine, astronomy, mortuary work. I've apprenticed with society's best dressmakers, for who better to educate me on stitching than that elite breed. I devoured all of their knowledge and I brought them here, into the dark where I've worked for four hundred years.

"I brought you back," I say, clearing my throat.

Though never vain before, I avoid mirrors these days. Not because they predicate a certainty that I am unattractive, but because my visage has become too much like theirs. My eyes, once prismatic, are merely green now. My hair is ink, calligraphic in architecture but ultimately banal, bereft of the iridescence that once ran venous through each follicle. And the planes of my countenance, the telemetry of their angles, even the crook of my lips, all these now suggest familial connections that I cannot yet observe without grief.

"You brought me back?" they repeat, voice feathery.

"Yes," I tell them, my vision clouding with tears. "In the taiga, you said to bury you, to carry a lock of your hair with me for all of my years. So you could experience immortality that way.

But I . . . couldn't. I found you in the ashes and I thought—I thought you would prefer this more."

Their legs are enamelled, pearled at the joints. I gave them pianist fingers capped with gold. But not hair yet. I had wanted to consult them on what they'd wear.

"How?"

"Slowly," I whisper, not trusting my voice to not break. "Too slowly."

They say nothing, clasping their throat with a hand.

"I'm sorry if this is not what you want. I can fix this. I can let you rest again. Or I can help you leave. I've amassed enough of a fortune in these years to assist you in beginning a new life. I can—"

Wordless, they unfold their arms, stretching them out to me.

There is no hesitation. I plunge into their arms.

And it is enough, it is more than enough.

Acknowledgments

Thank you as always to my editor, Ellen Datlow, who once famously opened an edit letter to me with the words "DON'T PANIC." (I did, in fact, panic, because jesus christ, there were a lot of edits in the letter. My god.)

Thank you to Kristin Temple and Kelly Lonesome for all the ways you've accommodated the fucking chaos of my life, for being good and kind, for being wise, for being marvelous editors. I am going to give myself imposter syndrome trying to live up to your sweetness.

Thank you to my tireless publicist Giselle Gonzalez, to the venerable Jordan Hanley, to everyone else on the marketing team, who were here before and who have come since. Holy hell, none of this would be possible without your work.

Thank you to Michael Curry, my long-suffering and deeply beloved agent. I want to say I'm going to be less of a chaos gremlin, but that's a lie and we both know it. I hope you still adore me anyway.

Thank you especially to Kyungseo Min, to Rosa Dahtler, to Thomas Beeker, to Ann Lemay, Brian Kindregan, Diandra Lasrado, Claire Cooney, Carlos Hernandez, to all you wonderful people I am able to call my friends and chosen family. I love every one of you.

Thank you to my Mouse. It's been twenty years of misadventures. I want decades more. Let's have as many as we can wring out of this world and the next. We're so going to hell, but at least we're going together. I love you. I hope you knew that already.

Lastly, thank you, Jeff. You are a weird hard-drinking chimney of a nerd, and I wouldn't have you any other way. Of all the books I have written and will ever write, this one feels most appropriate to dedicate to you. This book of mine about people who won't give up on each other, who stay even when the world crumbles to ash, who hold on even when there's nothing but hope.

I'm so grateful you're in my life. Also, I love you and now everyone who reads this book knows it too. So there.

And In Our Daughters, We Find a Voice

My prince kills my sisters before they can come to me, their deaths my bride price, the payment for an unwanted humanity. His fishing ships and his harpooners drive them into the rocks and the salt-whetted cliffs, into the maw of the coral. They chase them with nets and explosives purchased at great expense from China, until there is nowhere for my siblings to go but up, up into the searing blue air.

My sisters die voiceless in a froth of red foam, gasping mouths and gaping eyes, no different from common fish.

Then, when all the life has been bled away, when all is still and silent and there are only coils of drifting entrails, the ships lower men into the water to retrieve the bodies. The youngest are processed quickly; deveined, deboned, skins removed and crusted with salt and spice before they're left to dry under the sun; the meat carefully separated and stored in chests dripping with ice. The oldest they preserve with formaldehyde and meticulous stitching, with pins and steel rods and hooks no wider than a strand of hair, anything that can allow them to pretend that this was a crusade, not a slaughter.

Their trickery succeeds. The kingdom celebrates and my prince, he devours my littlest sister at his soothsayer's behest, marinating her first in cumin and cilantro. She was barely more than a fry, too young to emulate his idea of human. In a few months, that would have changed. Her skull would have flattened and grown sleek with long, silvery hair. She would have been beautiful, perhaps even beautiful enough to have taken my place.

"I saved you," my prince says as he picks the soft meat from her spine.

I say nothing, look down, pick through the kelp heaped on my plate, try not to think about the first time I saw my sister, peering from between my father's teeth, freshly hatched and clumsy, still viscous from the egg.

~

The ocean is not like the territories of man.

My father sends no armies in retaliation. My mother does not poison the seas with her grief. The fish do not mourn. Even the wind is silent, indifferent. Ten sisters are nothing, less than nothing.

~

He gives me no salt, only sugar.

Acres of caramel drizzled on pastries and baked into sinuous eclairs layered between crumbling shortcake and bittersweet chocolate. Endless cakes, all intricately made, some infused with strange fruit, others with crushed wildflowers and ginger. Scones dripping with cream. Glittering jellies. Macaroons and marshmallows and meringues fragile as hummingbird eggs.

Only once did he make the error of feeding me meat, a tender cut from the leg of his latest kill. Seven men died mangled for this mistake, that gift of power, and I almost, almost reached the shore before he snared me in barbed wire and dragged me away.

From then on, he kept me sequestered in a windowless room in the highest tower of the castle, buried in organza and lace, in books devoted to domesticity, in the green smell of the hills, and flowers that drown me in pollen every spring. My prince allowed me nothing sharp, nothing dangerous, nothing that could be used to cut or maim.

Not even my teeth, which he wears on his crown like a warning.

~

Occasionally, my sisters visit me.

They are not unhappy, for all of their new ephemeralness, their inability to taste or touch. Death has given them color, imbued their deepwater pallor with indigo and orange and filaments of gold.

They flick through my prison in iridescent circles, less tangible than a soap bubble. Though they do not say it, I think they're grateful they're not me.

———

"A queen should know how to write."

I raise a careful look between my lashes and smile at the doctor who'd spoken. My new teeth are blunt and perfect and white as salt, a strange weight that I cannot cease exploring with my tongue, like an old woman and a spiced knot of boiled sinew. The doctor could be male, female, a combination of both, or perhaps neither, a sexless thing unlike the prince.

"We will deal with that soon. For now, there are other concerns," my prince replies, sullen. He rubs more olive oil into my skin. Once, his touch would have made me nauseous, but I've grown accustomed to his presence, his endless attention. "I won't tax her. I'm already asking for too much. But soon."

"So, she is to be illiterate and a captive until you've begotten her with your spawn?"

He tenses his arm. "I am not a monster. The pregnancy is necessary. It will free her. It will—"

The doctor sighs. The sound whistles peculiarly through their mask, the top half of some dead bird, bruise-blue and sunset-orange. The doctor drums fingernails against the crook of an elbow, head cocked just so. There is no fear in their stance.

"Turn her into a proper wife?"

To my surprise, the prince supplies no admonishment, only a cold stare. I offer him no comfort, of course, a glance and little more. After everything that has happened, not even my father would be able to demand such an obscenity from me. So, instead I slope forward, leaning into my curiosity. Who was this person? And why did they dare to speak so boldly to my prince?

"But since you insist"—the doctor stares straight at me—"I suppose I should be the first to congratulate you on your fatherhood. The princess is pregnant."

In his euphoria, my prince takes no notice of my indifference, or the way the doctor tilts their skull one way and then another, as though to say they *know*. I touch my belly, press down. Under my fingertips, I can feel the myriad pebbling of a thousand eggs.

In my dreams, I see the Sea Witch, sometimes.

She is not terrible, not magnificent.

Just old.

It takes exactly three months for my condition to become unmistakable. In that time, my prince transformed from captor to curator, perennially hungry to discuss how he met and loved the mute girl he found on the beach, how he saved her from sea, how a new joy—a future, he gushed once—was now gestating in my belly. To display me where and when possible, on the balconies of the palace, in a banquet of dignitaries, anywhere so long that people can look and exult in our matrimonial glory.

"If we have a daughter, I can only pray that she is as beautiful as her mother," my prince declared to a company of neighbouring kings one night, his hand warm around my wrist.

Daughters, I thought to myself, as he joined our mouths, his lips sticky with mulberry wine. And they wouldn't just be beautiful, they would be clever too, and quick as a lie, and always so very, very hungry.

The first clutch comes too early.

I hide them in the jewelry boxes of a visiting countess. If the noblewoman notices her windfall, she makes no announcement of it. She leaves almost as she came, slightly richer but no less unremarkable.

Months later, they'll tell me of a haunting in a distant castle, of the salt-smell in its corridors and the figures in the spires, silks trailing from their skin like fins. Of how they sing so desolately, like birds who have never known the sky, or sirens exiled from the sea.

Everyone who is anyone knows the story of the little mermaid.

She falls in love with a drowning prince and surrenders her voice for a man who can't even remember her name. She walks on knives for him. She aches. In some versions of the tale, her sacrifice cuts her a kind of happiness. They marry. The story ends, and what comes after can only be presumed to be happy.

In others, they do not. Instead, he falls for someone else, a woman with a voice, a woman with property and the accoutrements of a noble title, a woman with value he can measure in parchment and gold ingots. The mermaid's sisters come for her in these versions. They give her a knife to cut herself free. In some endings, she does. In others, she does not, dissolving into a gasp of sea foam, forgotten except as an example, although of what, exactly, no one seems to know.

The stories aren't entirely wrong, but they're certainly not right.

"It's been a year." My prince paces the foyer like an angry tomcat. "An entire year. What's wrong with her? What happened to the pregnancy? She—"

"Calm yourself. This isn't about you," replies the doctor.

I catch my smile in my teeth, unwilling to bare emotion.

"No. It's not. It's about the child," my prince snaps and for an instant, I experience a frisson of what I can only imagine is love. He adores our daughters. Even though he has no knowledge of their physiognomy or their personalities, he is entirely devoted to them. "It can't—it can't be good for them to be inside her for so long."

"If she was human, no," the doctor tsks as they store their equipment in a leather satchel. "But the 'princess' isn't human, is she? I've checked her vitals. She's as healthy as a mermaid can be while being kept away from—"

"Stop." He massages fingertips into his temples.

The doctor stops.

"I don't want to hear any more of your nonsense. She is not returning to the sea. She's won't—she won't be a monster. She's human and she is mine."

"Yours," the doctor repeats. They sniff, disdainful. "And you're worried about her pregnancy."

My prince snarls. "What is that supposed to mean?"

"If you can't figure out the answer to that, Your Highness, it's not your knowledge to have."

Something is wrong with the second clutch.

The eggs are smaller than they should be, clouded, not crystalline clear. Their inhabitants sit motionless: tiny, barely more than a tendril of meat. As I arrange them on the sheets, my sisters in attendance, I weep. This should not have happened. They had deserved better.

As the sun bleeds from the horizon, brass and gold, molten, I devour the remains of my stillborn daughters. They are bitter. They reek of tragedy. The future will be better, I assure the rest of them, hoping against hope that the flesh of their sisters would be insurance against an uncertain tomorrow.

Everybody has a theory about where mermaids come from:

Sea foam. Goddesses, pale as milk. An act of spontaneous genesis, precipitated by a circumstance of oceanic currents. The semen of sailors dripped into the mouths of tuna. There are a hundred thousand million suppositions.

Only mermaids, who no one ever asks, are ever right.

It is time.

I squeeze my prince's arm and he startles, his free hand already groping for the sword he keeps on the bed. A curse loops itself around his voice as he migrates from sleep to awareness. I hold his wrist throughout. Wait. Slowly, his panic transmutes into concern, into dawning excitement as his eyes settle on the hand I have rested on my belly.

I mouth the words at him, hoping he understands. It's time.

And he does.

~

Gore spumes from between my legs. There is blood, blood, more blood than I had thought imaginable, brackish and thick. I scream, soundless. Unseen by my prince or his subjects, my sisters cluster around the bed, crooning reassurances, even as they slip, one after another, into newborn bodies.

The last of my daughters do not arrive in silence, contained in their eggs, delicate, vulnerable. They come shrieking instead, full of teeth and rage, full of power.

~

I stroke my fingers over the tatters of my prince's face and he gurgles, somehow still impossibly alive, his throat bulging with daughters.

The room drips crimson.

My children look up as I slip from the bed, their eyes shining black, their mouths razored and round. If this were the ocean, they'd be floating in the tangles of kelp, in their father's hair, darting between his teeth, safe, safe from the world.

But they're here instead, and we, like everything else in the world, will make the best of what we have.

I wait until they are ready, until all the noises have ceased before I open the doors and the windows, and watch silent as they spill into the night, hungrier and more dangerous than any prince and his kingdom.